THIEVES

Book One: The Obscurité de Floride Trilogy

GREG JOLLEY

Thieves

Book One: The *Obscurité de Floride* Trilogy

by Greg Jolley

Copyright © 2020 by Greg Jolley

All rights reserved.

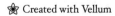 Created with Vellum

Dedicated to
Josh Evans, a good friend and fine surfer who showed me the
difference between fear and respect.

PART ONE

Steal a little and they throw you in jail. Steal a lot and they make you king.

- Bob Dylan

CHAPTER ONE

Tropea

LWR: *My partners will flame me when the money disappears.*
    April: *You have one hour to hit Send.*
    LWR: *Isn't there some way? Can't we...*

April wagged her finger in a child's *no-no* gesture at her cell phone beside her lunch plate of *lagane e cicciari* before typing again.

April: *Stop. Hit the key. Have your beautiful and strange life back.*
    LWR: *My files?*
    April: *As soon as the funds post, they'll be released back to you and only you. Not my call, but you've got the assets. No need to bother your partners. Just, what, sell a boat or two.*
    LWR: *How do I know you won't come back at me?*

April: *Because I promised. Gotta trust someone.*
LWR: *I'm a lawyer.*
April: *Nope. You're the shark in a kiddie pool. Fifty-five minutes.*

April tapped the conversation closed and took a sip of citrus water, using her spoon to stir the shaved ice. She stood, slid the cell phone inside her sundress pocket, and walked to the balcony wearing her headphones with the race reports turned off. Three stories below the rooftop apartment, turns seventeen, eighteen, and nineteen twisted downhill, a snake of narrow road between the markets and shops near the center of Tropea, Calabria, the race season's only stop in Italy.

Three motorcycles went through the first left turn slipstreaming, braking, tails wagging as the fat tires fought for grip. Their high-performance engines blasted and belched with compression as the riders worked down through the gears. Completing the turn, they were inches from the hay bales along the stone bridge wall, accelerating hard before leaning over so far that their knee guards kissed the pavement. The three fired down through the second bend. Mature trees blocked April's view of the short straightaway before turn nineteen where the three bikes pitched hard in the opposite direction, front wheels twitching, rear tires marking the road with wheel-spinning acceleration.

In the respite before another group of racers appeared, April looked out over the terra cotta roofs of the terraced city perched over the Tyrrhenian Sea. Shops and houses were packed in tightly and stacked and rising steep, most painted the timeless hues of parchment.

Balconies and rooftops were crowded with race fans, many sweeping the air with the flags of country or race teams. A dozen bikes in four-packs worked the downhill switchback. Not seeing Molly's colors, she left the balcony and went inside their apartment. The open-air great room had views of the Tyrrhenian along one side and the steep hills and wild olive groves on the other. The furnishings, like the ancient seaside city, were rustic, functional, and beautiful in basic design—dark wood for the walls and bookshelves and polished plank flooring with carpets and waving drapes of sunflower yellow.

April crossed and stepped out into the heat of the day under an endless blue sky and a fragrant breeze from the sea. This side of the hilltop apartment offered a view of most of Tropea, the densely-packed buildings and the long coastal Via Marina dell' Isola Boulevard, the highest speed section, a long-curved straightaway along the water where pleasure and fishing boats rocked in the low tide.

"Keep off the furniture, babycakes." *Furniture* was the racers' euphemism for hay bales, hedges, trees, lamp posts, and bridge abutments and balustrades. Molly was in the 500cc class, number 533, in her sea blue and black livery. A single rider flew along the straightaway at 235 km/h, followed by a pack slipstreaming, none in her sister's colors. Another group in a line screamed along the waterway, no blue and black leathers.

Signora Giordano, the sister's housekeeper, stepped out behind her with a spring basket of freshly cut blue violets for the veranda table. Placing the flowers in the vase, she arranged them into a blossom display, speaking to April with her eyes low to her hands.

"*Signorina Aprile, il computer sta squillando.* Miss April, your computer is ringing."

"Grazie, Signora Giordano. Did it sound like a slot machine spitting coins?"

"*Non capisco.* I do not understand."

"Right. A joke."

From the bottom of the basket, Signora Giordano lifted a pair of binoculars and offered them to April, "*Miss Molly è mangiare?* Is Miss Molly winning?"

"Dunno. I'm hoping she's staying upright."

"*Le mie scuse, non capisco.* My apology, I don't understand."

April tightened down her lovely blue eyes, mentally strolling through the nouns and verbs learned during the packing for this trip. What she came up with she knew was stilted.

"*Fiori belli. Si, un Tesoro.* Flowers beautiful. You, a darling."

The two women shared a kind, friendly smile like mother and daughter as their difference in age encouraged. April raised the binoculars and watched the fast motorcycles hurling along the shoreline. No sign of Molly, she set them on the table, touched Signora's arm kindly, and headed back inside, "She must be in the twisty sections."

"Si," Signora Giordano offered agreement rather than ask for an explanation.

"I'm thinking of going with cranky ditz or gum-smacking blonde, whatcha think?"

"*Cranky ditz?*"

"For the flight. Need to go answer the ringing laptop, pack, and clean up." April eased past the elderly woman, gracing her shoulder with a gentle brushing of her hand.

Her suite of rooms was to the side of the kitchen, through French doors of unpainted wood, the glass mottled by age. The laptop was on the low table before the couch where she sat and clicked the message icon. Having set the alert for messages from her offshore shell company, she frowned at not seeing the encrypted title reference to the bank. Instead, a previously set-up alert from US law enforcement could be made out from the numeric gibberish of the subject line. Disappointed but seeing the lawyer had another thirty-five minutes to pay out, she looked across to the open suitcases on the spare bed in the next room.

"I'm going with the gum-smacker," she decided, entering the second room and gazing into what she called her *looks* suitcase—wigs, makeup, her skin painting rig, and accessories. She took out a pair of intentionally bent sunglasses, two packs of Double-Bubble, and an iPod. Not seeing her *Meg* wig, she looked to the hall door, complaining, "Mol-ly!"

Undressing into the second suitcase, she walked naked into the bathroom and ran the shower. While it warmed, the pipes rattling and moaning, she pulled off her *Tiny Tina* wig and set it in the sink, looking herself over in the mirror just beginning to glaze with steam. She saw that her shaved head had started to bristle. "I'll shave back in the States," she told her reflection.

After showering, she dropped the *Tiny Tina* into the looks suitcase, set out her clothes, and pulled on a robe to go search Molly's rooms for her *Meg*. If her rooms had a Spartan techie vibe, Molly's room was all a chaos of dropped clothing, motorcycle parts in disrepair, and a dining table with a sprawl of hand-built skimmers and parts. There was also the smallest of hand tools beside the illuminated round magnification lamp. She stirred through Molly's *looks* suitcase before searching and sweeping aside racing and street clothing. Not finding the careless tangled, blonde *Meg*, she left the suite. "I'll go with the dirty brunette rug, good old *Bru*."

Signora Giordano spoke from the open kitchen where the rotary house phone hung beside the doorframe.

"*Il taxi sta arrivando.* Your taxi is on the way."

"Grazie, Signora." April made out *taxi* and *arriving*.

"*Signorina Molly vince la gara*? She translated that roughly to Molly and winning or leading?

"Not a chance, but she has the best style."

April slid the robe off her shoulders, and it pooled around

her bare feet as a flowery cloud. The gum-smack dress was already laid out on the bed from the night before, a gaudy silk print of oversized ripe fruit on a parrot-yellow background. Before pulling it on, she pulled the oversized shoulder purse of zebra stripes over and began overfilling it—maps, old Calabria newspapers, loose cash, cosmetic wallet, passport, unzipped laptop case, two fresh packs of Double Bubble, two slices of *cudduraci* pastry wrapped in paper cloth, and two bottles of San Benedetto orange soda. Stepping into two-inch heels with tropical colors and rhinestone patterns, she took up the *Bru*, bunched it up, and tousled it with both hands before putting it on her head and taking the laptop with her to the bathroom sink. With the computer open on the side of the sink, she did the familiar and careless makeup for the gum-smacker look and feel, giving her lithe and buoyant, pert-breasted figure a glance before opening Messages for a status on the wire transfer.

"Fuck a duck." She closed the laptop, adjusted the wig to add additional carelessness, and left the bathroom for the last time. Preferring to go sans bra and panties, April nonetheless put on both, purchased at the Blasa Cinzia boutique from the discount bin in the back of the shop, liking the ridges and frumpiness they added to the lines of the dress. From her makeup kit, she inserted one of her pair of dental falsies, providing a beauty-marring, unfortunate overbite. Pulling on a teal and lime travel jacket and the crooked shades and sliding the laptop into the floppy purse, she zipped up the two suitcases and left her suite. Although she and Molly had been living with Mr. and Mrs. Giordano for fifteen days, like most thieves, she avoided goodbyes, preferring to slip out the door and leaving it ajar for the cabbie to carry her bags down.

"Molly will do the *nice-nice*," she being the better mannered of the two. Most of the time.

The taxi driver took a circuitous route through the

narrow, steep streets to avoid the road closings for the race event. Passing through the Largo Villeta Tunnel, he steered April from the city and onto the airport highway. In the back seat, April used her cell to peek at the race standings. Lap eight of twenty-four of the eleven-mile temporary road course was completed. Molly was in P5 in her 500cc class.

Unable to check on the ransom payment on her laptop, she stared at the passing countryside through her open window filling the old sedan with the hot, fragrant summer air. The dry hills of olive groves were to her right, and the rock fields and yellow grass rolling downhill to the sea to her left.

"*Ti è piaciuto il tuo soggiorno a Tropea?* Did you enjoy your stay in Tropea?" The driver turned the music down and asked, looking at her in the rearview mirror, seeing the almost beautiful young woman with her bent sunglasses, amazing breasts, misshapen teeth, and a mess of mahogany shoulder-length hair swept back in the breeze. Getting no answer nor a returned gaze from what were surely beautiful eyes, the driver turned the music back up and concentrated on his driving. The race event had brought an overflow of outsiders to his home town, many unfamiliar with the roads and often drinking too much midday bottles of Donnici.

In the shade of the awning at Lamezia Terme Aeroporto, April paid and tipped the driver after he had unloaded her suitcases onto a porter's cart. She breezed through customs, eyes down, gum chewing, walking a little unsteady at times in her shiny rhinestone shoes. As always, she wasn't concerned with the faces she met. It was the CCTV cameras, which were everywhere, and the various agencies behind them.

She checked the board for the status of her and Molly's separate flights and entered the bar halfway to her gate. It was blessedly free of wall-to-wall televisions, and she felt herself being checked out and ogled and studied and fallen in love with. The Cocktail di Aeroporto was crowded, mostly traveling men in packs or single. She strolled to a round table and chair against the back wall.

The laptop woke quickly and synced with the airport Wi-Fi. She launched TOR access and was navigating to her banking when a carafe and two glasses were placed on the small table. Ignoring the drinks she hadn't ordered, she opened a second window to scroll her encrypted email headings while the TOR processed, the male chatter to her sides tuned out. No message from the lawyer.

A deep and swarmy male voice spoke from her side. "*Spero che vi piaccia il Cirò. Posso unirmi a voi?* I hope you enjoy the Cirò. May I join you?" She made out the name of the wine and guessed at *possess* and *you*.

"Nope," she said without looking up but closing her laptop for safety.

"Ah, *Inglese.* I have some."

"Then, you win, but I'm not the prize."

"*Scusa?* Excuse me?"

He sat at the table beside hers, laying his hat aside. April still hadn't looked up, even though her computer was closed. His paws for hands raised the bottle of Cirò and poured two glasses. He raised one in her direction, "*Alla bellezza.*"

April made out *beauty*, removed her shades, and let her lovely blue eyes work their melting charm. She saw what the fat hand and deep voice suggested, a large businessman with his necktie dashingly loosened. He took a sip and bobbed the glass to her, saying, "I'm Barbaro Agro. And you?"

April popped a stick of gum in and flashed her unfortunate teeth at the letch, enjoying the bug eyes and trembling, floundering of his confident, meat-eating smile. She pictured his mind as a house full of children like a brood of puppies in t-shirts, wifey with a mixing bowl in hand, glaring.

Her second glance at him told her immediately, showed

her, the furnishing of his mental home—equal parts a desk with stacks of money worries and a television running streams of porn with black and white photographs of wife and kiddies on the far wall.

"I gotta run." April blinked a smile, and taking out a debit card, placed it in the tab tray, knowing what he'd do next, which he did, placing his own on top of hers. She memorized his number and demurred, gently taking her card back, carefully tipping his over to capture the three-digit CVV code. Thanking him, she went to her gate.

Five minutes to boarding, she had TOR back up and saw no messages and no money wire from the lawyer. On her cell, she performed some deposits and transfers, saying to herself, "Molly's gonna go radioactive."

She texted two messages to her sister.

April: *A Mr. Barbaro Agro is paying for the apartment plus a generous tip for the Giordano's. He has also depleted his account with a donation to our fav charity.*

April: *Our pooch is screwed on the other thing. I have new candidates I'll start working back in the States. See you on the other side.*

On the laptop, she emailed the lawyer.

You're choosing money over your rep and career? Welcome to your personal but no longer private nuclear blast.

. . .

That done, she kicked off the migration of the folders. The lawyer's books, incriminating messages, and documents all floating off to the press, authorities, and surely the woman's soon-to-be ex-partners. Ten minutes later, April was in her preferred bulkhead seat with the extra leg space, her head resting on the round window, the blinds drawn for a well-deserved and peaceful sleep.

CHAPTER TWO

Swipers

On lap nine of twenty-four around the narrow and obscenely fast road course, Molly aggressively downshifted and squeezed off a blast of the throttle, kicking out the rear tire to pitch the bike for a faster line into the next turn. The bike in front of her was an early braker, going for smoother, cleaner lines that were usually faster than her aggressive wild style. She late braked, and with her abnormal wide handlebars giving increased leverage, locked her elbow to say, "cuse me." The two touched, bumped, the other bike wobbled, and Molly leaned all the way over, knee pad scraping the pavement as she passed.

Coming out of the bend sideways and accelerating, she aimed her sights on the three-bike pack 80 km ahead, her rear tire nerfing the curb which she caught and ignored, upshifting down the steep and narrow two lanes before the triple switchbacks of the Strata del Serpent. All four bikes went airborne over the knoll, suspension bottoming out on landing under hard braking. She ran down through the gears from fifth to fourth and skipped to second as the paving up the steep road changed to cobblestone. The four turned as one like train cars on the same line, engines screaming, balancing on the edge, fat black rear tires spinning and marking the cobblestones.

Each length of the switchback was a blast of acceleration before brake rotors glowed, and the riders lay their bikes over, this section so narrow that only one line was possible. An ageless stone wall was to their left with the steep drop to the city below. The turn at the top of the hill spilled out onto the straightaway across the ridge where if a rider were to look, he or she would see the sea through the flickering trees. This was where Molly lost pace because her engine didn't have the technology that the team riders enjoyed. She made up under braking into the sandy hairpin and by getting back on the power faster. She didn't get a pass but had closed up when the four entered the long swing turns unwinding down the mountain to the north. The road widened back to pavement as she entered the slipstream of the bike ahead. They snaked at 140 km/h, leaning left then right, the furniture of hay bales, lamp posts, trees, and curbside shops streaming inches from leaning bodies and high-powered motorcycles.

Molly was in fifth place, determined to get two more passes for a step up on the podium. Of the four ahead, one was in the top class of 750ccs and had broken free on the first straightaway, powering away from Molly and her 500cc group. She nabbed fourth place with a sketchy late braking at the 180-degree turn back to the city and lost it under the run down through the sway turns with houses and shops stacked high along both sides. She needed to recoup fourth before they got onto the long, bending straight along the seawall avenue Lungomare Guiseppe Gilardina, the 'Gil,' where horsepower would say what it always said. Between her and the killer long run was a series of seven squared-off, tight city-street turns, her best chance for a take or two.

She grabbed fourth place with her knee clipping a curb, inches from a post box, the bike ahead choosing safety over daring. Her bike wobbled, and she fought with the mustache handlebars and won and narrowed her eyes on the fat rear tire and exhaust of the next bike. Closing on the squared-off turns, she lost time on the block-long straightaways, streaming past shops, restaurants, and onlookers in doorways and behind waist-high concrete barriers at the intersections. The next opportunity for a pass was the tricky, technical three-turn 'S' where the pavement was dusted with sea sand. The bike in front of the pack of four bobbled and twitched under acceleration, and the group bunched, but she had no opening to take advantage of as they poured out onto the Gil, full throttle, snapping upshifts.

A 750cc team bike passed her like she had backed off the throttle to enjoy the ocean view. Flat out in sixth gear, the train of racers she was in stretched out, her at the rear losing meters to the factory 500ccs with their higher performance parts and tunings. The grandstands were a colorful blur to the right as the racers took the slight and wide bend onto the start-finish straightaway, crossing the hand-painted strip and entering lap ten of the eleven-mile road course. Another 750cc took her casually on the outside, and the only consolation was the plodding pack of 125cc bikes she tore past, easily 70 km/h faster. The straightaway ended with a mickey-mouse chicane where she got alongside the third-place bike but couldn't make the deal.

Back on the cobblestones, she made some ground as they worked the uphill doglegs before screaming out onto the treacherous Via Punta Safò with its insane sixth-gear bend, flat out for the brave and crazed, a lift by the wise and those who wanted to race another day. Molly came out as she entered, full throttle, stealing third place, and gaining her first *temporary* podium step. Pavement replaced the stones up the mountain ridge before turning back to the city and the downhill run through the tall warehouse streets, building faces right up to the curbs, casting the race with a sense of high-speed tunneling.

A tight right-hander spilled the racers onto Corso Vittorio Emanuele Avenue, which fed into the heart of Tropea. Two clicks along, the road rose as it crossed over the aqueduct. Molly and the other bikes went airborne at 120 km/h, all holding position in flight, focused on a smooth landing instead of taking a position. Crossing Via Indipendenza Boulevard, the pack entered the cobbled plaza with its church and shops, centered by the historical round fountain with canvas pillows lining the curve of the ancient carvings should a racer go errant.

Molly attempted another late braking into the next straightaway leading from the city. She got the place but lost it under acceleration. They ran side by side, the other bike inching forward as they approached the next sweeper. She let him go, so she could take a deeper outside line into the next turn, setting up for an inside, late-braking take. The other rider leaned nearly prone, cutting off her front tire, and the slight advantage she had taken. It was a good and effective block, and they came out heal to toe.

Her next opportunity was the ridiculously narrow double-turn flick taken in sixth gear, full throttle, no letting up. A few lunatics braved clipping the curb and grass on the apex before the oncoming 'sweepers' lined by ineffective hay bales before the edge-of-town cafés and shops. She was one of them.

A passing 750cc bike went by and slid wide from too much entry speed and nearly collected Molly. It was a brave or demented move, one that got the racer closer to taking the next position in his class *or* a page-three snapshot and head-line—another heroic death.

Her group stacked up for the fourth gear *flick* onto the next straightaway, a series of undulating high-speed blasts with twisting second gear late-braking turns, Molly's best section for overtakes. Coming out of a left-hander and running up the gears to 150 km/h, she and the bikes in front rose over a knoll in the pavement, all tires spinning on air before the suspension-crunching hard right. All four bikes made it through, twitching for balance and traction and forming back into a single line for the treacherous sixth-gear elbow 2 km up ahead.

On exit, the lead bike clipped a hay bale that launched it off the ground. The motorcycle smashed the coarse plaster wall of a corner bistro, the impact exploding broken, spinning parts, the racer pin-wheeling like a tossed doll up the roadway.

Going by last, Molly's bike was struck toward the rear by a piece of flying aluminum, stabbed in the spokes, thankfully, of the rear tire, locking it for a flash before tearing away. The fat rear tire streaked the pavement long enough to start the skid that Molly fought all the way until she clipped the side-walk curb. The bike, wobbling and low on its side and still accelerating, spilled Molly off and launched her. She flipped and tumbled twice before scratching on knees and palms up over the sidewalk as the bike crashed and wrapped around a lamp post. She smashed through another useless hay bale, sending up an explosion of dust and hay.

Laying up against the garden wall that brutally ended her loose-limbed skid, Molly lay perfectly still, seeing the wreck in a flickering of images while also attempting to inventory damage to her body. Thirty seconds passed before she sat up and looked back up the road.

Raising the visor of her helmet, she flinched as two bikes slipstreamed through that same turn where the other fallen rider lay just outside the race line. To the left, just around the corner of the bistro, orange fuel flames were pumping black smoke up into the yummy Mediterranean blue sky and tall green trees.

Getting to her feet, feeling a strange twist to her left arm and wrist, she ran up the sidewalk like a jittery squirrel beside traffic out of the racing line.

"Which one?" she questioned, her voice muffled by the helmet.

Her bike or the downed rider? The way the frame of her 500cc was bent and mangled with a pooling of fuel and oil-like blood saying enough, she jogged up the road where volunteers and marshals in orange vests were running like frightened children to the side of the still-prone rider. Yellow flags were waving.

Take a hardboiled egg and crack it on a table hard enough to smash it one-third flat, and you'd get the rider's helmet, a vibrantly painted, partially flattened brain basket. A train of bikes roared past at an eighty-percent pace for the waving yellows, honoring the flags but little else. Though muffled by her helmet, Molly heard the needlessly urgent wails of approaching sirens. Marshals were squatting and kneeling around the stricken, very still rider, wisely not touching, their expressions horrified and sad.

There was nothing she could do.

"Not gonna stand here like a worthless gawker."

She looked to her bike, or the *remains* of her bike, and walked away down the road. That's when she saw her bent, broken wrist. She watched three men struggle her bike upright and drag it up an alley, leaning it where it belonged, against a garbage dumpster, a stricken and mortally wounded machine. She left it there to be photographed or picked over by locals with tools for a quick wad of euros.

After a long walk back through Tropea with the screaming wails of the continuing race echoing off the terraced houses and businesses, she weaved through the team lorries and vans, through the mechanics and fans, entering the first team tent she came to, a simple awning beside a trailer. Being an independent, her place was located off to the side of the pits, her simple trailer on a patch of yellowed lawn.

With her good hand, she removed her helmet and wiped the sweat from her face with a rag from the first workbench she passed. Two plump and content men sat in canvas chairs with their rears to a smallish RV. They were either team owners or sponsors. A teenager in a team shirt stared at her from beside a parts and tools table. Molly unzipped her leathers and peeled them down to her hips. Stepping close to the boy, she borrowed a roll of duct tape, giving the gawking kid a little breast bounce under hard nipples inside her sweat-dampened silk undershirt.

"*Grazie, bello.* Thank you, handsome."

The youth's eyes left her breasts slowly, regretfully, turning to her efforts to wrap her dangling broken wrist.

"*Posso aiutarla?* May I help you?"

She studied him. It was her way to characterize people as vehicles. She thought, *A wannabe hot sports car, but sadly up on the blocks of unaffordable hope and lust.*

"*Grazie, no,*" she said.

She wound the tape four times around the wrist in two side-by-side lengths, handed the roll to him and ducked out from the shade and into the heat and glaring light. Her helmet in her good hand, she got her bearings and started off on the long walk and climb to her and April's apartment.

Signora Giordano greeted her on the landing at the top of the long stairs, plying a dishcloth with worry. Molly's thousand-mile eyes said no further conversation was needed, and she followed her recent guest inside and across the grand room to Molly's suite. Setting the helmet on a side table, Molly stripped out of the leathers, unmindful of the open door. She removed her race boots and peeled off April's fav *Just Fucked Meg* wig, all blonde tangles.

From the doorway, Signora Giordano offered, "*Fammi chiamare un dottore*? Let me call you a doctor?"

"*No, grazie.* I'll use my doc in the States."

When Molly dropped her panties, Signora Giordano left the doorway.

"*Per favore chiedere a tuo marito di salire e aiutarmi pack?* Please ask your husband to come up and help me pack?" Molly asked over her shoulder, pulling off the shirt and entering her bathroom.

While the shower ran and warmed and the full-length mirror fogged from the corners inward, she turned slowly, ignoring her lithe and ripe, beautiful and sexy body. She saw her injuries, the purple bruised hip and right ass cheek. Inside the shower, she stood back from the water, holding the bottle of bath gel in her injured left hand, squeezing out a gob and starting at the top of her shaved head, rubbing her skin downward. Stepping forward, she rinsed both her body and thoughts of the race slowly and completely.

"Travel role?" she asked herself as the suds swirled the drain. Visualizing her options, she decided to go with one not used in the past nine months, Miss Edge—a black mop, light blue eyes, painted pale skin and black tee, jeans, and unbuckled jackboots. After drying off, she closed the bathroom door and fired up her Norvell HVLP Handheld System and filled the canister with 'Moon Glow Creamy White' pigment. Five minutes later, her smooth caramel skin was a ghostly and ghoulish shade of bleached bone.

Pulling on the *look* in her messy and disheveled bedroom, she greeted Mr. Giordano in the front room, and the two packed up one of the trunks with her carburetors and bike electronics and tools. He kept his eyes on task, not daring even an arched brow at the completely different- looking American woman who left him to the motorcycle trunk while she bundled and stored her clothing in the other.

As Mr. Giordano struggled with the first trunk down-stairs, Molly filled a black backpack with her laptop, wallet, passport, and the various skimmer cables before leaving her rooms for the last time and going to the kitchen. From the icebox, she took out one of her three bottles of Stolichnaya and twisted off the cap. She emptied it into her travel thermos and went in search of Signora Giordano to express her and April's thank you and goodbye.

Down on the street, she also thanked Mr. Giordano, who was keeping an eye on her trunks until the shipping company van arrived. He smiled and handed her the lodging invoice.

"*Sì, lo farò a PayPal l'importo completo dal taxi.* Yes, I'll PayPal the full amount from the taxi."

Molly pocketed the bill and crossed the road, and a few minutes later, entered the dense celebratory throng of race fans among the food and souvenir booths, weaving her way leisurely to the main entrance. There were four skimmers to collect, one at the bank, and the others at the temporary ATMs closest to the restaurants and wine bars. The electronic overlays were of her own design and handiwork, devices she could mold and do the chip inserts most anywhere her motorcycle parts trunk was opened.

Using Miss Edge's grousing and frustrated husky voice, she removed one skimmer after another, saying over her shoulder, "The fucker's tryin' to eat my card."

Leaving the main gate, she hailed a cab, "*Aeroporto e veloce, dannazione.* Airport and fast, dammit."

After removing each chipset, the skimmer molds went out the window, spinning in the wind and dust.

By the time the taxi pulled to the curb in the shade of the departure doors, all four chips had been cabled and the data dumped to her laptop. Molly paid the driver, trash-canned the tiny electronics, and joined the tediously long queue for Customs. The line snailed forward as she read April's first text, telling her that a mark she had hit in a bar had covered the apartment bill and had been robbed. She scrolled to the second text.

"Fucking knew that 1-800 lawyer was sketchy," she said loud and cranky, startling the woman and boy in front of her.

She and her sister chose many of their blackmail victims off billboards in the States, lawyers with two-hundred-dollar hair styling and movie-star makeup. The faces often had an aggressively raised chin, a mark of confidence. They also went after the occasional cosmetic surgeon, chosen the same way, alongside the highways.

———

Forty minutes later, she was at her gate, boots up on a chair, her black shades on, looking bored and restless at her airplane parked on the tarmac with the accordion walkway attached. This leg of the flight was under-booked, perhaps twenty passengers also waiting for the call-up.

"Wrist looks bad," a heavyset man in a race-team shirt was lowering his wide ass into the seat across from her. She waited a moment before glancing up slowly, reading him decisively, *a fat truck with new chrome rims and engine not well maintained.* She stared right through his head as his cockiness melted, still taking in the mysterious, punkish, and lovely young woman.

The boarding was announced a few minutes later. Gathering up her backpack, she followed the queue aboard the airplane.

Sharing April's penchant for the extra legroom of the bulkhead seats, Molly opened her backpack between her knees while a university teenager settled in beside her. Ignoring him then and for the remainder of the flight, she tapped the service button overhead. When the steward arrived, she asked for three cups of ice and opened her first-aid kit.

The ice arrived while she chewed a Trazodone. Four OxyContins were next, washed down with the first of three cups of Stoli on ice from her travel thermos. The aircraft was taxiing out onto the airfield when she grinned at the sinking med and vodka stupor coming on, a flush at first, erasing her for the first of the flights back home.

She and April needed to be sharp when they regrouped in the States. Their business had taken a hit with the blackmail failure, not to mention the expenses of the race and travel and the bike build. Until then, she could hide and melt away from all their troubles.

CHAPTER THREE

Rick Ables, Jr.

Detective Richard 'Rick' Ables, Jr. arrived at the Tropea apartment early the next morning, missing the Danser sisters by more than thirty-six hours. Not his fault, the incompetent and greedy airlines had once again dog-fucked his best-laid itinerary. Having flashed his revoked US Marshal badge, he had walked and examined the girls' rooms with the Mrs. Gior-something trailing and complaining, her Italian sounding like tipsy Mexican. The rooms had been wiped and cleaned for new guests, and as he stood on the front porch looking down at the ancient and sun-stupid town, his lower throat gorged with the bile of frustration.

Descending the stairs to the street, he wiped sweat from his brow with the back of his hand, irritated further by the heat and air that felt mottled with sand and the smell of sea rot. He set the case binder on the roof of his pop can of a budget rental, unlocked the door, and climbed in behind the wheel. Syncing his SAT phone with his laptop, he opened the binder in his lap while a connection was made to his server back in Michigan. The first tab was the detailed chronology of the pursuit, which he updated with his pocket pen, characterizing the Tropea search as an empty gator hole. The laptop pinged, and he pulled it over from the passenger seat.

His slow-witted inside source had let him in on Molly's strange motorcycle racing life. Details from the search launched before arriving in this ass-up Italian town appeared as red flag icons on a map display. One was in coastal China in a city called Yantai. The second was near the Bristol shores in Britain. Doubting the girls had the juice to get into communist slant land, he did a search on the UK event, skimming the summary deep enough to see that the race was in two weeks.

"It smells right." He allowed his thoughts to rewind to the last time he was in Britain. "This whole nut sack began there."

Fourteen months prior, he still had a career with the US Marshals, working in FIST—Fugitive Investigative Strike Team—after flying a desk for six years in WIN—Warrant Information Network. His caseload was eighty percent military AWOLs who had chosen a life of crime, ninety-five percent of those dim bulbs nothing more than idiots with fast hands.

His prime case, the cream of the slop, was the hunt for the ugliest motherfucker he had ever seen. The clown had been on the losing end of a firefight for some bridge in Mosul, a failed attempt to retake the water supply where ISIS had shut it off.

Out there among the goat husbands, the bozo, fresh from the schooling at the M.L.I.— Military Language Institute— caught a flaming sack of munitions in the hands and face.

Looking like a blood-soaked mummy, he continued

working his scams while still in the hospital. He completed several of the sales like before—cash for ammo with the Danser sisters as go-betweens. Grafted and about half recovered, he slipped out of the hospital and made his way to Bitch One and Bitch Two in England, and that was where Rick, Jr. tracked him.

The sisters had him squirreled away in a country home outside of Farnborough. Renting a lorry, he parked it in a hedgerow a quarter mile from their hideout. Over the next few days, he became familiar with their movements, studying the long driveway and house with binoculars. Living in the van, he only left for food, braving the trips when a doctor visited.

During one of April's trips into the village for groceries, he approached her, all wrinkled clothing and unshaven.

The plan was to tell her about her two flat tires, chat her up, and offer her a ride home. He needed to slide himself slowly and deep inside her.

Before entering the market, he stuffed the ice pick in the garbage can out front. He found her in the dairy aisle, her grocery cart full.

"Hello, there," he said, hands in his pockets, a worried look pasted on his face. "I just witnessed a couple of punks slash your tires. I chased them off."

She gave him a quick glance and grinned.

"You're the sad detective living in the van. Seen anything fun yet?"

Taken aback, several denials raced through his mind. Her cool, confident gaze told him it was futile.

"Yes, I'm Rick Ables, Jr.," he confessed.

"Let me guess. Military police?"

"No, I'm with the US Marshals."

"You're far from home. Can I see your warrants?"

"I don't have them on me."

"Of course not."

Her beautiful blue eyes were taking him in, calculating, her smile never wavering.

"I'll take the ride home," she said. "You need to buy me two new tires. Here, play hubby." She nudged the grocery cart to him.

Taking it by the handles, he watched her turn, select two small bricks of cheese, and walk away. Rolling the cart after her, he struggled with how to play the situation.

Entering the bread and cookie aisle, watching her swaying hips and ass, he wondered if she was chatty in bed.

"Can I romance her?" he asked himself.

"Heard that," April didn't turn around. She took two loaves of dark rye off a shelf. "The answer is maybe. There's that whole thing about keeping your enemies close."

They didn't speak again until they were at the check-out counter.

"Let me get this," he offered, taking out his wallet.

"Good start, but no." She paid from a fold of euros.

Out front, she gave her car a quick look while crossing to his lorry. He got the door for her and stowed the groceries in the back.

Climbing in behind the wheel, he watched her put on a pair of sunglasses, making her all the more mysteriously seductive.

"I like the way you're looking at me," she said, casually resting her hand on his shoulder.

"You're a handsome man," she went on. "Tempting, even in your line of business."

Heading south out of the village, he was struggling, losing some of his focus because of the unplanned infatuation and fear that she was taking the wheel.

"We need to talk about the other... problem. I might be able to take some of the bite out of your situation."

"Yes. We'll get to all that later. For now, say something seductive."

"You're both smart and stunning."

"Good start. If it helps, I find you attractive. And the situation is certainly interesting."

He parked at the end of the long driveway in front of the house.

"Don't get out." She opened her door and began unloading the groceries onto the gravel. "Molly sees you, and you'll die right here. Let me smooth her."

A light rain began to fall. He watched her slide the door close and reappear at the passenger window

"Come back tonight." She ignored the droplets dotting her beautiful face. "Bring me chocolate or flowers, I don't care. And the warrants."

"Yes, tonight. Thank you, I..." he stalled out, knowing he sounded like some kind of love-struck kid.

She turned away, reappearing with grocery bags in both arms, walking to the front door.

Returning to the village, he rented a hotel room, showered and shaved and pulled on his last change of clean clothing. Sitting at the table under the window, he took his time regaining his wits. It also helped offering a prayer to his ghost.

Opening the case binder, he wrote.

Gather rock-solid evidence on the three of them.

Pull that off, and he'd get his career back on track, his suspension ended, his license restored. With those three apprehended, the investigators looking into his alleged financial irregularities would surely look at him in a new light and reconsider his explanation of the cash missing from the evidence cage. Same with the irregularities in his expense reports.

After spending an hour updating the case file, he called and had April's car towed to a shop for new tires. Before he left, he looked to the ceiling and asked for guidance. With no warrants, he'd have to verbally dance around that.

Leaving the hotel, he returned to the market from earlier and bought a bouquet of red roses and a heart-shaped box of chocolates.

Arriving at the house at sunset, April was standing just outside the open front door, bathed in amber porchlight.

"I've decided..." she greeted him, "... let's have ourselves a whirlwind seduction, a cloistered romance."

His holy ghost whispered words of caution. Looking her over, seeing her mischievous smile and eyes, he batted the warning away and offered her the flowers and candy.

"Set those anywhere." She took his arm and led him inside. "I've got something to show you."

"Which is?"

"All of me." She tiptoed and kissed him deeply.

Her bedroom was in the rear of the house, past the kitchen, a large room with drawn curtains and a four-poster bed.

"Is your sister home?" he asked.

"They're somewhere around here."

"I'd like to—"

She hushed him, breathing over a raised finger before unbuttoning his shirt.

———

Four days later, he forced himself to come up for air. They had spent their time together living and dining in her bed.

After two days, he gave up on asking about Molly and the soldier, finding that the topic turned her to ice. That's also when the detective's holy ghost left him out on his own. He fell in love with April. Her sleepy bedroom eyes, her ready smiles, her spilling tits, and bend-me-over requests. They ate and showered together and only turned away from one another for sleep, April needing to cocoon herself with the blankets on her side of the bed.

When they talked, April steered them to his line of work, finding it interesting and asking flattering questions, drawing him out.

At one point, Molly joined them in the kitchen, carrying an empty breakfast tray. She was all catwalk, caramel skin, beautiful eyes, and a dangerous, far away smile. She looked him over and laughed.

"Don't mind her." April kissed his jaw, whispering, "She's got brain damage."

"Heard that." Molly smirked and left.

That last morning, he awoke to an empty bed and a silent house save his ringing cell phone. Sitting up in the tangled sheets, he looked for April, guessing she might be in the bathroom.

Calling out her name, there was no reply.

His phone rang again. Seeing his supervisor's phone number, he let it roll to voicemail like the others.

Climbing from the bed, he tapped on the bathroom door. When she didn't speak, he padded out to the kitchen. She wasn't there, either.

An alarm began sounding, softly at first.

Returning to the bedroom, he pulled on his pants and wandered the first-floor rooms. Not finding her, he went up the stairs. The door to Molly and the soldier's bedroom was open. The bed was made, and there were no personal belongings anywhere.

Ten minutes later, he had searched every room in the house.

"April?" he called, already trying to process and accept what the silence said. She had played him, all the while asking questions about his work. Screwing him to madness, she also stole his heart and picked his brains clean.

Going out front, he sat on the porch. Seeing no cars but his own, he took out his phone and listened to the last message.

All he heard was 'last chance' and 'Get your ass back to the Arlington as soon as yesterday.'

————

Back in the states, expecting a spanking, he was drummed out of the service so fast he was standing alone in the parking lot at eleven in the morning. His career was dead and buried, all his successes tainted. He left headquarters with a hefty severance check which was a good thing because during the days and nights with April, she or Molly had emptied his checking and savings accounts.

Walking out to his rental car, his holy ghost returned and perched on his right shoulder, its razor-sharp talons stabbing into the open sores from its last visit.

"You let that bitch take everything," the ghost accused.

"I know that," he answered out loud, something he rarely did.

"Time for you to nail her to a cross. She and her sister and the soldier."

"Working on that, now piss off."

Driving back to the airport, he struggled with how to locate them without the resources of the US Marshals.

Pulling into the line of cars at the rental car return, he opened the case binder and flipped to the third tab, labeled, 'Molly Danser.' On the left side were the pages of his report before being sacked. To the right was the single page of details on her describing her as five-foot-six inches, one hundred and twenty pounds. No visible scars or tattoos. Hair and eye color—various.

He stared at the photograph for the thousandth time. There was her elusive and stunning beauty, her dreamy, sleepy eyes *almost* to the camera. There was also her thin, perfect nose and just a glint of a wise-ass smile. When this photo was snapped, she was painted a gothic pale, accenting her expressive, rose lipstick.

Tearing his eyes away, he saw the gravy-fat black girl and her belt-attached computer waving him forward into the vacated spot so she could check the mileage and whatever else. Ignoring her, he braved tab four, 'April Danser.'

Seeing her photo, the ghost clenched and jabbed its claws deeper, causing him a jaw- clenching stab of pain. Looking into her intelligent and sparkling eyes was like pouring ethanol alcohol into the talon wounds, filling the deep tunnels boring into his skin and muscle. In this snap, she was airbrushed a Caribbean tan, almost cocoa, and beautifully failing to regain control of sincere laughter, her sunglasses crooked on her perfect face, her hair a mess of raven locks.

The country-fried girl rapped on his window with her fat knuckles.

"Pull it forward." He read her lips.

Setting the binder aside, he slid his computer onto his lap. Firing it up, he launched the hideously expensive hack he had bought off the dark web. Miles of code spilled down the screen before coming to a stop at a series of options. He chose B, which read, 'Freeze.' Clicking on it launched an ice age on one of the sister's recently discovered offshore accounts. It was a start. Next up was locating them.

There was an aggressive rap on the window. Rick lowered it.

"Fucking hold your water," he chewed at her, not making eye contact.

"Screw you, horsehead." She mocked his long-jawed, otherwise handsome face.

He climbed out, elbow ready to fire, but she wasn't interested, focused on greasing her rotund body in on the seat to do her thing.

———

Fifteen minutes later, he was in the terminal taking a seat in the ticket counter lobby.

Setting the binder aside, he reopened his computer and ran a then illegal search on the farmhouse in Farnborough. With a few minutes of digging, he was looking at a facsimile of the rental agreement.

"There you are," he whispered, recognizing the handwriting of the signature from long ago. The name was a fake, of course. The face associated with it went way back, no matter that it was hideously burned. His troubled history with the soldier cut deep, and seeing that handwriting opened long-buried memories.

Running with the false name, he dug deeper using pirated software from work.

"This smells right," the ghost encouraged him on.

It was true. A thread from the name led to the airlines.

The trail resembled the foul and soiled droppings from one of his three elusive fugitives, and it was enough to move forward. Unlike the sisters who knew better, the soldier had fucked up, booking a flight in the same bogus name used on the house documents.

"Well, won't cha look at that." He memorized the arrival date and time.

Seeing the destination, he closed his eyes and grinned.

"Ready or not, cunts, here I come."

CHAPTER FOUR

Clance

The long black car navigated the late-night airport queue, pulling to the curb under the cruel sodium lights before the second set of arrival sliding glass doors. The sidewalk was sparse, only a few jetlagged travelers standing in stupors beside their suitcases, staring blankly into the arriving headlights.

April spotted Molly inside the terminal, dropped the passenger window, and waved. The glass doors slid open, and two airline employees and a security guard guided Molly's wheelchair out of the chilled interior and out into the warm, humid night. Her sister was slumped over and snarking at the three trying to help her.

"Again?" April frowned while climbing from the back seat of the hired Lincoln town car. The driver got out and circled to assist Molly from her wheelchair. She got to her feet, a helpful hand on her elbow and another taking up the courtesy blanket, spilling a half dozen tiny liquor bottles. Molly was gently spilled into the back seat, handing April her backpack, trailing the scent of alcohol. April climbed in beside her sister.

"How's Clance?" Molly said slowly as the car pulled away.

"Fine. Up to the usual."

"Mean the unusual?"

"Yes. Getting a CNN erection, eating catered delicacies."

"Who are you this evening?" Molly squinted.

"One of Clance's favs."

"Deranged, mouthy Tina. Been a while."

"It makes him happy. Keeps him calm."

"Have the driver stop. I need ice."

"Will do. The wrist?"

Molly raised the taped wound-swollen wrist. "I'll have it set after a forty-eight."

At the next exit, the driver steered into a Quickee parking lot, went inside, and returned with a seven-pound bag of ice. April helped Molly refresh the remaining vodka in her travel thermos before emptying the remaining ice onto the pavement.

Back on Highway 94, Molly sipped from her straw as April slid her laptop from the backpack to check the skimmer proceeds.

"That can't wait?" Molly asked. "What about some chummy time?"

"You get yourself forty-eight hours of sleep, and we'll have a dance party."

A half hour later, the town car entered the long sweeping bend onto Highway 23, bypassing Ann Arbor to the south. Rolling north at a leisurely eighty-five miles per hour, the girls ignored the streaming spruce and poplars lining the road, bathed in flickering highway lights.

April scrolled through the miles of skimmer data, doing quick calculations in a side window. "Well done, Mol."

"Thanks. Have a new bike to buy."

"That bad?"

"Wrapped around a lamp post."

"Explains the wrist. Sorry, I know that race was important to you."

"Yep." Molly raised the makeshift cast. "There goes the Bristol Shores 200."

April did a rough total, guesstimated expenses, and said, "The net is good."

Just past the exit for the notorious and crime-ridden town of Dent, the driver performed a smooth, blinker-free pass on the inside of an eighteen-wheeler. A mile and a half later, he slowed for the Wildwood Lake exit. Deftly passing a slow-rolling pickup halfway down the ramp, the car kicked up shoulder dust, dry grass, and road litter.

"He drives like you." April looked forward.

"Fast, but not *even*."

Past the stop sign, they turned onto the main drag, passing shop windows blackened for the night. To their left, the lake appeared between the bungalows, a flat pane of still, oily water.

"Slow up. Don't wanna wake the yahoos," April told the driver, and he lifted off the gas and kept the vehicle to the posted twenty-five miles per hour, tipping the nose of the car at the town's single stop sign. He slowly rolled them the next sleepy mile before the right turn onto the dirt and gravel North Shore Lane.

"Find any new barrels?" Molly asked, meaning 'of suckerfish.'

April's preference was for wealthy 1-800 lawyers and high-flying cosmetic surgeons for their ransomware hijacks.

"No need. I'll work the list we already have."

North Shore Lane undulated with the terrain, feeding narrow dirt driveways in both directions to cottages and lake cabins. The moon and sky were unavailable with the tree bows overlapping up above as the long car navigated the twisting up-and-down turns. They came to a stop on the weed lot next to 9514 Shady Way, the lakeside residence alongside the local joke, the Wildwood Lake Country Club, which was nothing more than a fire pit and three picnic tables before a shared dock. The thin-faced house was of weather-worn wood shingles, front and sides. It could say rustic or sad and old.

The driver got Molly's door, and she slid out onto unsteady feet, April swinging around the car to wordlessly pay him by peeling off cash before taking her sister's elbow. As the town car started up, the girls crossed the shallow driveway to the side of the dark house and went down the side steps to the lawn between the back porch and the lake.

Past a pair of beach chairs and a tire rim fire pit, they brushed past the limbs of a wide pine tree and walked the simple dock of old, skinny planks. Passing the owner's collection of kayaks and sailboards, the sisters approached their worn and rust-spotted pontoon that April paid the homeowner for docking privileges.

Getting Molly seated in a plastic deck chair near the front, April untethered the boat, sat on the bench seat behind the wheel, and started the outboard. After reversing twenty feet out across the shallow water, she turned and upped the throttle, the boat aimed toward the middle of Wildwood Lake.

"Running lights," Molly said.

"Oops, right." April turned them on.

Thirty minutes later, the only boat on the lake had crossed the still and silent waters to the row of shore houses on the east side. Slowing to a crawl, April steered into what looked at first like an impassible tangle of poplar branches with a carpet of lilies. The pontoon eased forward, the limbs brushing the aluminum side rails as it entered the canal of stacked stone walls.

Both girls ducked time and again as the branches brushed past, the narrow water running straight except for one ninety-degree turn. Passing under a wooden bridge, the stone walls widened away before the boat rolled out onto the chained lake. April nudged the throttle, and they motored out onto Horseshoe Lake, bordered on three sides by state preserve lands. To their left was a row of five lake homes on the east shore peninsula. April brought the boat to a stop in a slip cut into the seawall running the shore at the base of the last home to the right.

As soon as April had Molly up onto the steep lawn of their house, the two climbed while sensors kicked off stunning security lamps all around. Their place was a seventies' tacky track style house that looked transplanted and airdropped from suburbia.

"I'll get a doc out here tomorrow," April said, taking out her ring of keys.

Molly didn't reply, her head down from the brilliant lawn and tree lamps.

They had bought the place furnished. The interior was like a seventies' time capsule of walnut surfaces, heavy and ornate furniture and walls, and details painted burnt sienna and avocado.

After tucking Molly into bed with a glass of water and two Trazadones, April went down the hall, carrying Molly's laptop downstairs to the unfinished basement.

The long, dark room was faintly lit by the little blue and green blinking lights from the servers and racks of network equipment. Setting the laptop on her battered roll-top desk, she switched on the desk lamp. Cabling and syncing it with her computer on a side table, she sat in her rolling chair long enough to remove her boots and socks. Staring at the cobwebs stretching across the open beams above, she reconnected with her brashy Tina role before heading upstairs.

She left the sunporch and went down the hill on the other side of the property to the eighty-foot dock reaching out to a blackened houseboat sitting patiently in the warm night. The air was vibrant with the flavors of moss and fresh-cut lawn. When her barefoot stepped onto the first board, the sensor illuminated the houseboat from all sides, the lights cast from two poles. Stepping aboard, she unlocked the side slider door and entered the dark interior.

"Hey, boyo, I'm feeling all clammy inside. Gooey-like."

Clance turned from the open refrigerator, a bottle of pop in hand, the interior bulb painting his scarred, ruined face in cruel pallor.

"Got a roll of quarters for your Vibromatic," April said, looking at the hanging beads that were Clance's bedroom door. "Shall we?"

Clance closed the refrigerator and crossed the room, twisting off the bottle cap. Leaning down and kissing April's neck, he asked, "How many quarters you bring?"

CHAPTER FIVE

Dance Party

After her forty-eight hours of sleeping herself sober, Molly strolled down the lawn and along the dock watching a solitary swimmer trailing a 'V' of ripples. The far shore of state land hills and trees were painted golden by the lowering sun. With her good hand, she held a rolled-up *Café Racer: Bikes & Parts* catalog. Wiping her black work boots on the mat set out before the houseboat's walkway gate, she called forward, "Ding a ling."

Clance leaned around the corner of the house.

"Permission to come aboard." He grinned, stretching the scar tissue around his mouth and cheeks. He was wearing swim trunks and an apron.

Molly walked alongside the stern deck and was welcomed with a kiss on the cheek.

"How's the wrist?" Clance asked. Her left arm was

restricted by an elbow cup-to-palm fiberglass and aluminum rig.

"Dry hump this thing. Fuck being seen wearing Velcro," she raised her wrist where the grip fabric crossed in two places.

"Miss Edge, I assume?" Clance took in her gutter mouth, the *Moe* wig, and wrinkled black silk dress unbuttoned to her navel. The left sleeve had been torn off.

Molly gave him a tight glaring eye. "Missed you," she said insincerely.

Clance laughed. "Almost mosquito hour. Want some spray?"

"They wouldn't dare."

He took a long-neck lighter from his apron pocket and circled the rear deck, lighting the surrounding citronella candles in glass bulbs. Molly took the white plastic chair beside the back door.

"Something to drink?" Clance circled the small space and stood with his back to her, hand shading his eyes.

"You know better."

A small open launch was coming in slowly from the south, keeping a safe distance from the swimmer by hugging the shore.

Five minutes later, the caterer's boat arrived. As soon as it was unloaded, it departed.

April swam in slowly and climbed the rusty swim ladder. She stood smiling at her sister while water ran from her blue and white checkered summer dress. Her blonde wig was done up with odd-angled ponytails, and her sensual body showed through the fabric. She wasn't wearing a bra or panties, and the dress was nearly transparent.

"A towel, Cupcakes?" Clance offered.

"Nada, Sweet Toy. Let the sunny sun do its thing. Time for din-din?"

Clance went inside to set out dinner, leaving the sisters watching each other.

"Better?" April asked.

"Some. Shopping helps." Molly raised the racing catalog.

"How long till you can ride again?"

"Doc says six weeks. Means three."

"You can rest up some more when we get home."

"We're leaving when?"

"Dunno, gotta finish smoothing Clance."

"He'll come. He likes your smell."

April laughed and nodded in agreement.

The sisters went inside.

After their Dixie plate dinner, the three sat facing the lake in the waning light, the air blinking with fireflies.

"You solid?" Molly asked Clance.

"Down to my last eleven thousand. I'm good. Setting up another ammo theft off a national guard base. Danser your real name?" Clance asked, studying five geese paddling by.

"The fuck that come from?" Molly bit back.

"Far left field."

April was ogling Clance's strong muscled body, sculpted from pale clay, staying mum.

"We got it in Provo," Molly said.

"Provo, Utah?"

"You think? Where else would there be a Provo?"

April spoke up, staring at Clance's molded chest.

"We were little girls, living somewhere in Los Angeles. Foster folks drugged and rented us. This man was supposed to drive us to another Hollywood party, but we woke up out on a desert highway. He was a good guy, no creepy stuff in the motel. Bought us food and let us watch the television. Then he started sniffing a rag from a tin bottle, and when he was out on the floor, we lifted his wallet. Got *Danser* from his

movie studio ID and library card. And some of his cash...
well, all of it."

"Florida, Clance?" Molly changed the subject.

"Yea, but not right away."

"We'll throw you a party," April enticed.

"I *do* like parties. With this face, I'm always a hit, making
everyone else feel handsome."

"See? Oh, the fun you'll have," April said, wiping sweat
from her temple, ear to the shoreline crickets chirping and
frogs croaking.

"Maestro?" Molly asked, and Clance got up and went in
and turned on his record player.

When he came back out, he reclined on a plastic lounge.
Salsa poured from the speakers, the volume cranked, the first
song dramatic, quick, and sultry. The sisters were to their feet
instantly, sensually swaying and playing their hands and shoulders, dancing with each other.

With the start of the second song, Molly and April were
beaded with sweat, eyes closed, fingertips sometimes coming
together in dance, hips and tummies bumping.

During the pause between songs, Molly opened one eye.

"Clance's got a boner smile," she quipped and winked.

The sisters eased into the next upbeat song, working it as
the music swayed out over the lake. April's bare feet and
Molly's black boots tapping and bouncing, their arms swaying
and raised while in pirouettes.

The album ended after the fourth song, and Clance went
inside to flip it over.

"April, your thingy's purring," he called out.

"And I thought we were outta quarters." She smirked.

"The other thingy."

Molly danced in the silence to the swim ladder and
lowered into the water, her black dress blooming before she
dunked under.

April retrieved her cell phone from the coffee table and started scrolling and reading. The music began, and she called over to Clance. "Cut it." Walking out back, rereading the alerts, she sat down on the front edge of Clance's lounge, shoulders locked, glaring down.

Molly climbed out and reading her sister's cruel eyes, sat down beside her.

"Our bank's been hit. We're frozen," April said.

"Which one?

"The only one."

"Weren't you going to scatter our monies?"

"Didn't get to it."

"How bad?"

"All 700K."

"Fuck. Who?"

"You're right, that's the important question."

"I can read this one. Shit news." Clance took the chair by the door.

He was ignored.

April closed the phone and looked ready to throw it.

"Time to open the briefcase bad?" Molly asked.

"Might be."

Molly went inside.

She stepped along the kitchen island of knives and guns and a rifle. Opening the freezer, she reached in past the boxes of ammo. Twisting the neck off an icy bottle of Tanqueray, she called out, "Got ice?" There were no trays.

"Yes, in the cooler by the front door."

Molly rinsed out a plastic cup and half-filled it with gin before crossing to the front door.

"Molly, think about it. Please don't," April called.

"Done that."

The record player was turned up, and Molly sashayed out into the evening dusk, cup to her lips.

"Seen this movie too many times," April told Clance. "Sometimes the forty-eights don't take. I gotta run. Enjoy the show."

April left to work on her computers in the basement.

CHAPTER SIX

Strip Malls

Early the next morning, April brewed a pot of espresso and took a tall cup with extra sugar out back and down the lawn toward sunrise over the lake. She sat down beside Molly, who lay sprawled on the grass with a floral chair cushion for a pillow and a beach towel for a blanket. Pressing and twisting the cup until it stood on its own beside her sister's outstretched right hand, she studied Molly for a minute. No sign of life except the bending of grass blades from her breaths.

"Oh, lost one." April got to her feet and walked down to the dock to the houseboat, finding Clance waiting for her with two cups of coffee, sitting in the light of the rising sun. The two had talked on the phone late the night before, and Clance was ready to go, keys in hand. She took the offered cup, and they sat silently side by side sipping before the smooth-as-glass water.

Fifteen minutes later, they were in Clance's pickup, April with her beach purse of reserve cash and a marked-up map in her lap.

Over the next nine hours, they bought four used big engine vehicles, Clance checking the tires for good tread and testing the motors while April did the deals. After each purchase, they stashed the cars near the red circles on the map across two different townships.

Back at the house, Clance headed down to his houseboat to order dinner, and April went in search of Molly, finding her in the basement. Molly was a twitchy, shaky knot of nerves rather than dried out, but focused, never mind the teeth-chattering mumbles of regret and remorse. She had wiped the dust off their battered and old Samsonite briefcase and sat before it, oiling and cleaning their guns.

The two worked silently for a half hour, April at her computer encrypting and migrating data from her and Molly's laptops to their Carbonite cloud. When they were done, they headed upstairs. Their reserve collection of outfits, makeup, and wigs were secreted in the locked walk- in closet of the master bedroom. While the sisters stood in the center of the closet, Molly spoke for the first time since the night before, rummaging through the hanging clothes.

"I'm going with Hicky, the ugly crack ho."

"Nice. Think I'm going British. I want to swear like Shakespeare."

"Name?"

"Victoria?"

"Vicky?"

"Vicky, sure."

"Hicky and Vicky."

They partnered on the details—eye color, choice of teeth implants, and wigs. They worked separately on their costumes.

"How many stops?" Molly asked, carefully considering her choice of running shoes or boots.

"I mapped ten, which means six or seven. We need to leave by eight in the morning. Take it easy tonight?"

"Nope, but I'll stop early."

"There's my girl."

April's cell phone purred with an incoming text. 'Dinner' appeared under Clance's name.

————

After dinner and dancing on the houseboat, Molly went up the lawn to the house for a fresh bottle of alcohol and never returned.

Clance reclined on his favorite lounge with his knees up and wide, cupping April's shoulders, her head back on his chest, the two sharing a cup of Fanta grape soda. The record player was scratching along the final groove of the last song. The evening was mid-summer hot and humid with no breeze, and the two were content and slick with perspiration, the sun low in the East.

"Florida?" April nudged lightly.

"Wouldn't miss the chance to see your homes. I'll head down as soon as I wrap things up here." He kissed the back of her head and brushed two fingers along the curve of her shoulder.

"When are you two leaving?" he asked.

"Soon as we get to the fourth car."

"How far is the drive?"

"Eleven hundred and thirty-five miles."

"Not sure that one's got the legs."

"Thank you." April turned and kissed Clance's muscled upper arm. "We'll replace it once we're out of state."

Five gray and white geese were crossing the water thirty

feet out from the stern rail. Studying their languid and dull search for bits of food in the shallow water, Clance kissed April's head a second time, saying," Let me up, and I'll go turn on the AC."

"Kay. I'll go up the hill for a roll of quarters." April smiled to the geese.

"Better idea." Clance got to his feet. "Lay in my arms and tell me about how fine life will be in Florida."

———

At six the next morning, April brewed espresso in Clance's kitchenette and carried a cup up the dew-cooled lawn. She found Molly lying face down on the couch in the front room, a bottle on the table beside a bucket of melted ice. All the blinds were drawn, and the room was frigid cold, the AC cranked. April sat on the coffee table and whispered across, "Rise, beautiful, it's a workday."

Leaving Molly with the espresso, April went to shower. Molly joined her a few minutes later, and the two washed up in silence before padding to the walk-in closet in the master bedroom where they dropped their towels and did cosmetics and chose wigs and eye colors. April finished up first and left in her costume. Waiting for Molly, she sat on the front porch in the shade of the stately willow tree, using her cell phone to call for a ride. Clance came up the hill to wipe down and clean the house and padlock the basement and walk-in closet.

Molly joined her, and they sat watching the road at the top of the driveway. The Lyft ride pulled in ten minutes later, and April gave the driver directions to their stop in Redford in the outskirts of Detroit.

During the forty-minute ride, the sisters talked only in banalities, both test flying their respective accents. Hicky grumbled in jittery gutter mouth, and Vicky enjoyed her

British accent by making naive observations of the low passing hills and industrial parks.

"The countryside is breathtaking, love, don't you think?"

"So done with pole dances. My snatch's worn and tired."

With the Lyft driver paid off, the sisters stood on the crumbling sidewalk on the north end of a sketchy and weary strip mall, Molly in her filthy wig, drug-tramp look, and insert of bad and missing teeth. April wore a straight wheat wig held in a bow at her neck, black sunglasses, running shoes, and a deep blue greatcoat.

Their first hit was the corner liquor store, the air ripe with Indian spices, tobacco, and the sickly-sweet hint of spilled alcohol.

"Favor me, my man," April told the hundred-year-old cashier in a turban. "All the cash and no conversation, please."

His eyes never left the Glock in her hand as he emptied the register and thoughtfully placed the cash in a plastic shopping bag. April elbowed Molly, who was watching the rest of the store with her back against her. They left and turned right, strolling without a word to the next mark four doors down, the Redford Tavern, a dark and sad dive with four early drinkers along the long Formica bar.

It was Molly's turn. Gun in her bad hand, she splayed her fingers on the bar, palm up in front of the unshaven bartender in a stained jockey shirt.

"Trick or tweak, fuckhead. The cash. Fast."

The man looked down the bar along the faces of drink-stupid customers.

"Ain't none this early. They're all tabbers."

Molly raised the gun barrel, aiming for the middle of his chest.

"I said *fast*."

He complied, keying the register and laying ones and fives

and tens on the sticky bar, saying only one word before stepping back, both hands half up.

"Cunts."

Molly let that go with a display of her ugly and discolored teeth while pushing the bills into the pocket of her trashy white fur jacket. With an elbow to April, they left without a word, April leading the way down the sidewalk past a green and gold Check 2 Cash shop to their first ride parked in the gravel lot at the corner.

Molly drove, and April navigated. Five miles up the forever long Eight Mile Road, they went by a local bank. As it swept past, both said in unison, "Grape," a reference to the time they had tried a bank and had been rewarded with a blast of ink packs that splattered the interior of the car and their clothing and skin in Kool-Aid purple. That had occurred during the second of their two strip mall jobs, way back when, their backs up against the wall by low funds.

The map led them along the backstreets of what looked like an urban warzone. The road was battered and uneven, the pavement cracked and pockmarked with potholes. Along both sides were rundown shops, most with gaudy-colored, smashed-glass business signs. After a series of turns among shuttered storefronts and houses, April pointed.

"There."

Molly pulled in and parked, leaving the keys in the ignition, the engine running.

It being April's turn to play announcer, she pressed against the glass case with her gun out, staring down the Korean proprietor of the Go Ha Market standing at the register. A young girl and infant sat low to her side before a television.

"Good morning, luv," April said to the slack-jawed, wide-faced woman in her fifties. "Be so kind as to neatly stack all the cash in the register, and we'll be on our way quick as punch."

"Quick as punch?" Molly questioned over her shoulder, looking up the single aisle of the market.

"Sounds British, right?" April stared down the woman.

"Kind of. Your accent's good, though," Molly said.

The squat, gray-haired woman folded her arms across her chest and let loose a strand of foreign words, looking defiant and tired.

"*Now*, you churlish, hedge-born, maggot-pie." April aimed the gun at the girl and baby.

"The fuck that come from?" Molly giggled.

"Downloaded the Shakespeare Insult Kit." April glared at the woman opening the register.

April scooped up the cash, saying, "No need to stack it, love. There's not enough."

The sisters hustled down the sidewalk past a nail salon and laundromat to their next ride, a 1991 blue two-tone Buick Regal. Before putting the car in gear, Molly ran the wipers, sweeping hot dust off the windshield.

So far, there were no sirens nor any bug-eyed witnesses. Molly steered away at a leisurely pace, ear to April's directions.

"How much?"

"You know it's bad luck to count before we're done. But so far, *dismal*."

The sun was halfway up into the hot and hazy sky. They drove for twenty minutes, the windows down, the AC spewing nothing but a misty vapor.

———

It was now Molly's turn, so she entered the tavern first, good hand in the pocket of her glittery sequined short, short skirt, the gun shape clearly defined in the tight fabric. Adding twitchy, blinking unfocused eyes, she shouted, "Empty it, dickwad!"

At her back, April stared down two black men sliding slowly from their bar stools. Her gun was also out, held at her side, barrel rising. The men sat back down as Molly swept up the cash, and with an elbow to her sister, led the way outside, April pointing to the green and rusted Ford pickup at the edge of the lot.

Four blocks up, they whacked another tavern and the liquor store two doors down, this time spiriting away in a primer-gray and parrot yellow former taxi.

"That's it for Redford. We'll jump on the 96 for a half hour," April instructed, talking Molly through the streets to the highway ramp. This ride had good AC, never mind the sticky vinyl seats and a hearty loud motor. Molly ran the speedometer up to eighty-five miles per hour, the standard pace on all Michigan freeways.

April had her jump off on Grand River in Brighton, where traffic crawled along, constant stop lights running the main drag with name-brand stores on both sides. Four tedious miles up, a series of turns led to a backroad paralleling warehouse and trucking yards. They came upon a run of gas stations, quick marts, and boat and auto repair shops. A frontage road led to their next mark, CJ's Grill and Cocktails.

The place was half packed with an early lunch crowd. Ignoring the cutie at the hostess podium, April led the way to the registers at the end of the bar where a cluster of wait staff was ringing up tabs.

"All the cash and cards, dearies." She pulled the gun from the pocket of her greatcoat and got their wide-eyed full attention, "Hurry, please. Don't make me break out in Shakespeare."

They were in and out in under five minutes. Four blocks

up and two in, April pointed out their next stop, an ABC Warehouse Liquors.

Inside were six cash registers. The store was close to deserted. Bad teeth clicking, gun in her shaky hand, Molly barked at the two cashiers as one, "All of it. *Fast*."

Tills were opened, and two paper bags of cash were handed over without a word. There was a pause. April glanced over her shoulder. Molly was considering a tower display of green Tanqueray bottles. Molly grabbed one and started for the door.

"Really?" April maintained her British accent.

"Really."

———

Ten minutes later, they were parked in the angled spaces before the glass wall of a grocery store, the windows displaying images and prices of food and sundries. April led the way inside Polly's Market, a worn-out 50s' time capsule. It was a smallish store made ineffective by the chains. There were three registers, each with a gray-haired, *almost* retired woman, and no customers before any of them. To the left on a rise was a cigar-chewing, balding, and stocky man looking down upon his turf.

Molly exposed her gun and stared him back into his chair as April spoke to the first blue hair at register one.

"It's been a day, dear. Do me a kindness and be quick." Her gun was also out.

She carried the plastic shopping bag of bills to register two, saying in her best flowery lilt, "Hello, my mewling, fen-sucked, puttock if you would."

Molly sputtered laughter, and April grinned as well, her eyes never leaving the woman's old and hurried hands inside the cash drawer. Stepping along to the third register, she didn't flinch when Molly shouted at the man up in his perch.

"Hands back up!"

The cotton candy-haired woman began sliding cash from one tray slot at a time and forming a loose stack on the counter.

Neither April or Molly saw the other guy, a handsome, tired-looking big man in a Polly's shirt who resembled the owner but for a few decades. He eased his hand behind his back while rounding an aisle display, tight eyes alternating between the two sisters. Before his hand was halfway around, Molly spotted him, shouting, "Gun!"

April pivoted to her right, seeing the revolver rising. Her gun came up, swinging away from the cashier. She was two beats slow, his gun was on her, his finger sliding into the trigger guard. She swung hers and aimed at the center of his chest.

"I will," she screamed.

He aimed too fast and fired.

The blast was deafening.

April didn't flinch.

Already cocked, she pulled the trigger.

The man in his Polly's shirt was knocked backward off his feet, crashing into a wall display of chips and snacks before crumbling to the floor.

Molly dug her claws into April's upper arm and yanked, and the two ran amidst the shouts and echo from the gunshots.

They never got to use stashed car number four.

CHAPTER SEVEN

Killer on the Road

The yellow and primer former taxi got them as far as some bland-named town in Ohio before the temperature gauge went into the red, accompanied by a foul-burning smell from the floorboards.

Parking a few blocks back from a strip of used car and truck dealerships, Molly hoofed the half mile, leaving April slumped across the back seat.

Their next ride was a midnight blue Mercury Grand Marquis, long and wide and fast. Molly coddled and assisted her sister into the rear seat, and they got on the road, Molly finding an on-ramp without April's assistance, leaving the prior vehicle running behind a minivan in front of a tired residence.

Running south across endlessly flat Ohio, a stream of dullard town names passed by. Traffic across the state ran at a sheepish seventy miles per hour.

At their first stop, Molly wiped and pressed their two handguns deep into the filling station trash can. While the tank filled, she went inside for a tall cup of strong burned coffee and three packs of beef jerky.

Back on the road, she set her cell phone on her upper thigh and let it figure out their route and talk her through the highway exchanges. With April silent in the back seat, she let her thoughts turn briefly to the past. Twice in the past twenty years as thieves, they had been broke and desperate. Both had fired many hundreds of rounds at body silhouettes at gun ranges. Neither had ever shot at anything living.

"Enough on that." She took her first sip of the hot foul-smelling coffee.

"How we doing back there?" she asked over her shoulder, checking in on April's state of mind.

"We're trapped in the life."

"Try a cry?"

April took off her shades and gave Molly a one-eyed knife jab. Laying back down across the seat, she spoke up in a hushed, wounded voice.

"I pulled the trigger."

Molly let that float, twisting the corner of her lips, considering ways to help her sister forward.

"If you hadn't... both of us could've died."

"I didn't even pause to think. Just aimed and fired. I'm going to sleep now. Please keep talking."

Molly knew from their life together how her sister processed dark situations. April always escaped in slumber when faced with misfortune.

"We're halfway across Ohio. The state where foot doctors retire."

She blinkered and eased into the fast lane.

"Ohio *spawned* bestiality and barn murders," she said, hoping for a rise.

"Gave us retarded weather and gray miles of dead crops." Molly looked out to the endless countryside rushing past.

"Ohio, land of college football lunatics, tractor races, television addicts."

She cocked her ear to the back seat.

"Ohio gave us Ed Gein and AA."

That stirred April.

"Ed was from Wisconsin. Plainfield," April mumbled.

"Gotta be a typo."

"Good night, Molly."

"Good night, April."

———

A half hour outside of Ohio, Molly jumped off for gas and a drive-thru coffee. The miles wore on, her cell phone displaying the balance of their estimated seventeen-hour run.

Feeling the ghost of her hangover and road stupid, Molly crossed through a couple of states, hearing the cell phone announcing each. They became confused in her mind. West or East Virginia? South Kentucky? Shaking her head to clear such unimportant considerations, she focused on the fuel gauge and the road out before the long dark blue hood.

When the Grand Marquis died, it did so without a gasp. It went silent and kept rolling long enough for Molly to catch an off-ramp and coast to a stop. To the left was a rise of paving going up over the freeway bridge. To the right, a road ran into a strand of pines in low-rolling hills.

In her short, short glittering skirt and white fur jacket, there was no need to put out her thumb. She raised the hood and leaned her rear against the driver's door.

A man in his forties pulled his AC and Heating van alongside and hand-cranked the passenger window down.

An hour later, Molly owned a new ride, after negotiating

briefly with the owner of an auto repair shop. Another Mercury, this one a 1987 four-door dull silver Topaz. She used two of the credit cards stolen at CJ's Grill and Cocktails back in Michigan.

With April nesting in her blue greatcoat in the back seat, Molly ran the Topaz gently up to speed, listening for suspect engine strains and watching the gauges. They crossed another state, the name quickly confused, the cell phone showing they were two-thirds of the way home. Scanning the roadside signs for a Starbucks drive-thru, Molly called over her shoulder.

"Jerky?"

"Sure."

"There's my girl." Molly smiled up into the rearview mirror and handed a pack over the front seat.

Molly drove, and April slept, and the miles and the hours unrolled like a gray movie premiere carpet. South through both Carolinas and into Georgia, the pre-dawn air swirling in through the windows was sticky and hot and ripe with the scent of the dense roadside pines.

Five miles into sunrise—a low orange orb in the trees tossing cool shadows—Molly blinkered off the highway and aimed east to the sun coming up over Florida. A run of two-lanes wove and turned, the speed signs lowering until she was motoring along at twenty-five miles per hour. Miles of wild palmetto stretched out to both sides as the road wandered along a canal of royal blue water that ran only inches lower than the roadway. Two turns in, they entered the shade of tall oaks with draping moss reaching out overhead. The tires splashed twice through the high-tide overrun. The air was stagnant at times and always overheated.

After turning onto High Bridge Road, the next speed limit sign asked for ten miles per hour, and the first breeze off the Atlantic offered a gift of crisp sea scents. They came upon a queue of four vehicles at a temporary stop and blinking red light.

A deep, long note of a horn blew, and the drawbridge rose for an approaching fishing trawler.

"That our siren?" April sat up slowly and looked to Molly.

"It could be," Molly said. "We'll be home in twenty minutes."

The boat passed, the bridge lowered, and they drove the remaining few miles before a sand-curbed right-hand turn onto A1A. The miles south had palmetto and scrub brush to the right, and beautiful small blue waves brushing the beaches to the left.

Houses on storm pillars began passing, each a cool pastel green, apricot, or shades of coral. The beach to their right ran undisturbed except the wood beach stairs every quarter mile. Further south, the first strand of tall condos appeared, each also painted a welcoming tropical hue.

Molly slowed for the street sign for Windswept Road and turned in on the straight one-lane pointed to the Halifax River a half mile back. Halfway along, she stopped the Mercury at the chained start of their driveway, a thin run between the dagger-like explosions of wild cabbage palms.

She climbed out into the heat, unlocked the combination lock and idle rolled in, the tires hushing on the crushed white coral and sand. Their driveway came to a stop at a T. Molly's house was to the left on the river. She turned right and drove the car to April's place on the ocean.

Parking in the shade of the awning between the garage and the side door to the home, sensor lights coming in quickly.

"Let's get you poured into your bed. I'll go home and call in groceries for us."

April studied her house, chin on her crossed arms on the back seat.

"Thank you," she whispered, staring.

"Rest up and then get to work, please. I know it hurts, but there was nothing else you could do. Figure out the freeze and who did it and how to get our money back."

CHAPTER EIGHT

Clance

Ex-Marshal, Rick Jr., sat in his rental car at the Detroit airport, laptop open and cell phone in the crook of his neck, the AC blasting, chilling his sweat. The call to his last remaining buddy at the department finished as his eyes scrolled the lines of data he had cajoled out of the marshal who ended the call with an edge in his voice that said clearly, "This is the last time."

Rick Jr. migrated the data to a spreadsheet and launched a search for 'Danser' on the thousands of Michigan property title records. There were four, which was curious for such an odd last name.

He entered the first of the four addresses into his phone's GPS and drove from the rental car lot.

The first two properties were both in Southern Michigan and no-gos. No cars in driveways, the windows shuttered, no signs of life.

Number three looked like the jackpot. No sooner were his front tires in the first few feet of the driveway when grueling bright sensor lights lit the rental car from all sides, overheating the already hot midday. For such a simple boring house, the security was over the top.

The carport was empty, but he found fresh oil drops before ignoring the front door and looking for a low window to crack. Climbing in onto the kitchen sink among cracking shards of broken glass, he scanned for the alarm control box, the house sirens baying like a wounded banshee. Not having the passcode, he used wire cutters to snip the lines to the two alarm horns.

Silence fell fast, and he climbed from a kitchen chair in the AC-chilled front room.

"Maybe not," he frowned. The furnishings were rustic and cozy and clean, saying *retired couple* and nothing about Molly and April.

He did a room by room.

Seeing the padlocked master bedroom closet raised his spirits. Using a crowbar and hammer from the utility room, he went to work on the wall and door around the lock, bashing away plaster and wood until he had a rough carved circle. After a handful of shoulder and kicks, the door scraped open.

"Wa-la." He stood with tools in hand, looking over the odd clothing and wig racks and extensive collection of open cosmetic and theatrical makeup boxes.

The rest of the house was a bust until he went down the cellar stairs after destroying another door frame and solid oak door. Two laptops were cabled to a third computer on a table. He sat in the leather office chair in the warming glow of the password-protected computer monitors.

"Not surprised." He looked away, seeing a somewhat familiar and old Samsonite briefcase. "But on the right trail."

The briefcase was unlocked. He opened it and scowled. It was empty.

Back upstairs, the empty refrigerator said one word, "Gone."

He halfheartedly rummaged through all the drawers and bookcases and any paperwork he could find throughout the house, looking for a scrap of information suggesting their whereabouts.

Standing amid the spilled drawers and books pulled off shelves, a frustration headache was coming on. Clenching his teeth to drive it away, he glanced out the big bay window.

The lawn descended to a dock on the lake, the gray boards extending out to a houseboat, glimmering sun rays sparkling off the chrome in the hot daylight. The floating home was still, and all the blinds were drawn.

"Worth a look." He was discouraged but went out onto the back porch and down the lawn, passing a floral pillow and vague impression in the grass. Halfway down to the lake, his spirits rose. Music was playing from the otherwise dead-looking houseboat.

His first step aboard set the craft to a slight rolling yawl. He took out his Glock from its hip holster.

The aluminum door was unlocked, and he stepped inside rich, cooled air and darkness, except for bulb in the kitchenette and the blue and red glow from a large television playing CNN. A recliner was facing the news, and the top of a head showed. To his right, the single bulb cast light on the caterer's delivery boxes atop the four burner rings of the stove. The large room was filled with dramatic Latin America salsa shit. Ex-Marshal, Rick Jr., grinned for the first time in five or six days.

"They're not here, whoever you are," came from the recliner. "Got a warrant, by chance?"

The voice was calm and relaxed, and Rick Jr. holstered his

weapon before circling the big chair and sitting down on the facing coffee table. His nose scrunched upward in disgust, seeing the other man's ruined face. Looking away, he spoke.

"Hello, brother, talked to mom lately?"

———

Clance looked into Rick Jr.'s long-jawed facing, shaking his head one time to sweep away some of the long-standing hatred. His older brother took out two pairs of handcuffs and tossed them into his lap.

"They were for Cunt One and Cunt Two."

"*Jr.*, wash your tongue."

"Vagina One and Two. Better? Still stealing ammo with them?"

"I'm working those solo."

"Cuff your ankles while I toss the place."

Clance did so, leaning forward.

"The other pair go you know where." Rick Jr. stood up and scanned the room, spotting the record player and turning it off.

Clance cuffed his wrists after lowering the television volume with the remote. He listened to his brother muttering while trashing his kitchen and desk. Rick Jr. parted the hanging beads and called from the bedroom:

"Vibromatic? Always wanted one. Mom always got you the best toys."

"Oh, lookie here," followed a minute later, "Treasure under the mattress."

"Jealous snoop as always, Jr."

"Call me that again, and you'll lose your spleen."

Rick Jr. came back into the front room holding a pillowcase and Clance's passport with airline tickets in the fold.

"Daytona Beach International? Gonna go play butt buddies with the girls? Which one you boning this month?"

"Ex-Marshal jumping to wrong conclusions as usual. I'm going for a meeting with my military contact."

"Uh-huh. Quite the meeting. Six weeks by the date stamps on the tickets. Am I gonna get their address out of you?"

"You know better than to ask."

"I'm in a new mode, bro. No more going dot to dot, leaving sources like yourself to muddy the waters up ahead."

Rick Ables, Jr. went out on the stern deck. Opening the boat box, he took out a coil of boat line and went back inside with a five-gallon can of outboard fuel.

"Ever get tired looking at that face of yours? I do," Rick Ables, Jr. said. "No more *tee-vee*, time for a splash of reality." He placed the pillowcase over his younger brother's head.

Binding Clance to his recliner with the boat rope and securing it with a double knot, he sat back down on the coffee table.

"Your holy moly isn't..." Clance spoke through the pillowcase fabric.

"Holy Ghost."

"Isn't gonna like you anymore if you do this."

"Well, no, he's inspiring me. Setting things right. Justice and all that."

Rick Ables, Jr. stood and poured a circle of fuel around the recliner before emptying the rest in the kitchen and bedroom.

Returning to Clance, he said, "Bet ya still have a strong dislike of *that* smell."

"You thought about explaining this to Mom?"

Rick Ables, Jr. let that go without replying.

"I'm thinking there's not so much as a Bic lighter in your

home. Good thing I brought these." He took out a box of kitchen matches.

"You do this, the Marshal Service is gonna hunt *you*."

"Probably, but I bet I'll finish this first."

"Are the sisters worth losing your life?"

Rick Ables, Jr. took out a wood match and paused for no known reason, looking at the record player.

"Interesting question. Did they dance for you, too?"

"You won't get within a mile of Molly and April. They'll outsmart you first, then squash you like the insect you are."

"That's one version. A bit dark. I like mine better." He crossed to the front door and stepped out into the brilliant heat and daylight.

"Your holy spirit will abandon you," Clance called out, his voice calm, resolved.

"All this negativity and doom is making me tired. I hope your afterlife improves your attitude," the ex-marshal replied.

He struck the match.

When he got into his rental car to drive away in the evening light, the houseboat looked like an island of fire.

PART TWO

Impostor Syndrome: (also known as impostor phenomenon or fraud syndrome) is a concept describing high-achieving individuals who are marked by an inability to internalize their accomplishments and a persistent fear of being exposed as a fraud.

~ The term was coined in 1978 by clinical psychologists
Pauline R. Clance and Suzanne A. Imes

CHAPTER NINE

Isadora Flenc'

Molly woke to the sound of machinery and power tools and familiar male voices shouting and laughing down below. She hadn't made it to her bed and raised her head from the couch, looking along the trail of her clothing across the plank flooring of her loft. Her home was a single room with no walls that stretched across the entire third story of Klave's Boat Repair Shop and Storage building.

When she had first moved in, there was a brief child's delight with the visual of riding a bicycle from her bed to the kitchen and from the bathroom to her work area. April had bought her a garage sale beach bike for her birthday a couple of years before. So far, it had not come off its kickstand.

The path of her clothes led across to the side of the elevator where her and April's two open trunks from Italy had been set after delivery. On the low table before her was an empty bottle of Tanqueray and yesterday's special-ordered *Ann Arbor Times*.

"Can it," she groused at the workmen, knowing they couldn't hear her, rising from the couch slow and gingerly. She peeled off wig glue and stepped bald and naked into her shower for a quick rinse off of the previous night's drinking antics, knowing she'd take another before dressing for the afternoon charity soirée at the Halifax River Yacht Club.

Not bothering to dry off, she padded across the rough boards to her work area, an array of work tables covered with computers and exotic printers, mold machinery, and a refrigerated glass case of tiny electronics.

A batch of the current style skimmers lay fresh from the molding printer, ready for chip insert. There was a half dozen of the new model she and Allison cooked up which she planned to test fly the following day. The new ones were Wi-Fi capable, meaning no need to retrieve them for the card data. The wafer-thin skimmers were shaped to accommodate the various ATM manufacturers' designs.

Inserting the chips under the lit magnification lamp, her fingers a little twitchy from drink, she set the units for that day's work aside. Using two 2008 Miami phone books, she randomly fingernailed two first names from one and two last names from the other. She plastic printed two new driver's licenses, one for herself and the other for April. Placing the skimmers and an ID in a small purse, she went to the two trunks beside the gated elevator.

Unpacking her and April's skin paint rig, she decided to go with a deep cocoa tan and the red-mahogany stir of tangles wig, coming up with a nouveau-riche princess character. She showered a second time, sprayed on a face and full-body tan before selecting a revealing satin black cocktail dress and small accents of expensive, clinky gold jewelry.

Taking the rear stairs instead of the elevator, she entered

the first floor of the boat storage area where her motorcycle engineer, Allison, was at work in their shop space back of the stored and trailered boats and yachts. In front of her three draped cars, Allison was busy working off the VINs on the car she had bought with stolen credit cards on their way down, the plates already replaced.

"How they hanging, Ali?" Molly leaned over the fender and gazed at his efforts with the dashboard VIN stamp, watching him through the windshield.

"Tight as winter chestnuts," Allison replied, not looking up from his fingers and hand tools. "You want to sell or trash this one?"

"Sell. We need the cash."

Liking, as always, his British accent, Molly once again visualized the type of vehicle his mind was—an unpainted Porsche Carrera, the passenger seat filled with manuals, the car's engine and suspension high-tuned. A young man in his twenties, brilliant with racing motorcycles, he was on a slow rebound from his former drunken days. He was also merrily willing to help Molly with the skimmer electronics and most any other aspect of her criminal life.

"Hold off on the new bike order?" Allison plied up the VIN plate and set the replacement in place to be mounted.

"Yes, hold off, but go online and select the parts and electronics. April will be back up and running soon."

"Will do. Have yourself a day."

Molly left their work area and strolled through the storage boats to the front of Klave's, letting the voices of the mechanics draw her along. Passing through the repair area of dismantled engines, motor cranes, and parts shelves, there was the open two-story rolling door. She pulled on her black sunglasses against the heat and the tropical blue sky.

David Klave was with his guys, taking a work break with a round of icy beers at the table in the shade facing the blue-running Halifax. Out on the slow and smooth-rolling river, an immaculate, white power yacht was powering past.

Klave noticed her first and paused, he was the only one standing. The others turned and drank in the seductively beautiful Molly. David Klave was a stout and big-shouldered man, deeply tanned, his Klave's polo shirt freshly pressed. His deep black shining pearls for eyes revealed pleasure and wit as they took her in. *His brain vehicle was an immaculate, shiny, and black strong Suburban.*

The boat repair and storage company was a clean-money business, solvent in boating season, less so when the tourists waddled back north. As he liked to say, "Some months you eat the crawfish, and some months the crawfish..."

His mechanics went quiet as one to marvel, half of the eight employees in love with Molly, the others only wanting a half hour in a shower with her. Even with the heat and humidity, she was looking *sooo* cool and fresh.

"Skin like smooth chocolate butter," was whispered at the table.

"Thank you." She flashed a flick of a smile to Ronaldo, a familiar face.

"Mile-long legs and that rack," the emboldened blond mechanic, Dennis, chimed in, and Molly and the others shared a laugh, shaking their heads at his usual blunt ways. Dennis was the lead engine guru, his face a peach-red tan, his mind a hot rod with too many window decals and an under-sized engine.

Molly circled over to Klave and took his arm, walking him to the edge of the shade.

"Who are you?" he asked, eyes gentle and smiling.

Molly opened her clutch and stirred through the new skimmers, taking out that day's ID and took a peek, "Isadora Flenc'."

"Izzy? Like sparkling wine. I hope you're off to snag some hearts and wallets... bills are backing up here."

"I've got a full day charted. I'll be hanging with the rich and dense."

"Ever hit a country club? Gotta be the land of fat wallets?"

"I'd never even dance with a man who plays golf. It's worse than a silly sport. Mentally constipated and frustrated men seriously chasing little white balls with clubs."

"Subtle as usual. It was just a thought."

"Thank you. Today I'm working an exclusive shu-shu party at the Daytona Hilton and then an evening in the hot night spots." Meaning placing skimmers and nicking whatever credit cards that came available, using her and April's flip and memorize technique.

"The cast won't slow you down?" Klave asked.

"Not a beat. Even adds to my look of a wounded rich ditz."

Klave's eyes narrowed in appreciation of her model-beautiful face, no matter the black shades. "Be careful..." he smiled fondly, "... we need you on your sharp edge. The till's almost empty."

Molly made a mental promise. Absolutely no more than four gin and tonics. Squeezing Klave's dark muscled arm, she headed back through the building.

Allison raised the rear rolling door, and she headed off for work in her shimmering white Cadillac ATS-V Coupe, focused on getting the coffers refilled. She and April and the boat business were down to around nine thousand dollars, barely enough for two weeks' expenses.

———

The following morning, Molly woke up and took in her surroundings.

"Made it to the bed. Yay, me." Seeing black grease hand marks on her tummy and good wrist, she sat up far enough to confirm that whoever the lover had been was gone. Her brain felt twice its size. Clearly, she had again had more than absolutely no more than four gin and tonics.

"Robot, make espresso," she spoke toward the kitchen area as if she had such a contraption.

Washing her bald head and body in the open-air shower, the ghost of a moneyed, male body, the lower half, and a face with no eyes, swirled in her thoughts briefly but quickly rinsed away.

"Got us a short day," she recalled. Work a fru-fru charity lunch at the Halifax River Yacht Club before a gallery opening at four o'clock down on Beach Street in North Daytona, then over to April's to check-in.

After pulling on the Izzy look again, she emptied her clutch on the worktable, seeing that she had retrieved only two skimmers the night before. "We're going with the Wi-Fi units today," she addressed her drunken lapse the night before.

Down in the rear of the building, she casually circled her Cadillac, hoping to see no damage and relieved that the car was even there. Allison joined her, holding an open laptop.

"Spec'd out a new racing frame and new carburetor management system. Bit pricy, but very fast and blinding responsive."

"Good, you. The best. I'll be placing the Wi-Fi's today. Look for the data, please."

"They'll work. Good take last night?"

Molly grimaced. "Haven't peeked, but I was in all the best places."

"I cleaned the upholstery." He nodded to her white Cadillac coupe parked at an odd angle between her late-model pickup and nondescript gray four-door sedan. "Looked like Wrestle Mania was held in the back seat."

"Darling you. Thank you. Off to work I go."

———

Returning home that evening, Molly used the remote to open the rear rolling door and drove in out of the heat and light. Allison was nowhere to be seen, and the silence and shadows from upfront said Klave and crew had also called it a day.

Up in her walk-in shower, disjointed memories of the past hours played. A few credit card flips, and reminiscent of her daring teen days, two purses on chairs cleaned of cash and plastic. A dance floor with swimming soft blue lights. Wealthy male dance partners and a bone- thin matriarch with diamonds dangling from her neck, wrist, and fingers, a seductive and eye-to-eye slow dance while a quartet played.

Not bothering to dry off, she pulled on black sailcloth shorts and a slinky black silk shirt and black boots. She made a tall drink in a thermos and went back downstairs with her purse and the *Ann Arbor Times* from two days prior. From her and Allison's motorcycle build area, she rolled out the gray Vespa he had modified for her. The rear wheel well and front fender had been modified to accommodate the wider knobbed sand tires. The muffler had been removed in favor of a loud and more efficient exhaust.

Button opening the rolling door, she placed her thermos of iced gin in the cup holder Allison had mounted on the handlebars. Newspaper stashed in the back of her shorts, she drove out into the blinding heat and onto the path of sand that winded through the cruel knife-edge brush toward the Atlantic. She took the bike up to speed quickly, enjoying each turn of rear-spinning tire spraying dust on the ever-threatening blades of palmetto and thorn brush. The path took a couple of fine dips and rises and a shovel-built long banked turn before she opened the throttle wide, grinning at the brushing sea air on her scalp. Passing the gate road to their property, she raced through the turns of the remaining quarter mile to April's home.

CHAPTER TEN

Surfing in Church

April heard Molly unlock the back door and pulled off her black silk sleeping blinders. She lay stretched out naked on her vanilla leather couch before the wall of louvered windows filled with a view of the sea and the sky.

"How's April?" Molly asked.

"I'm busy, piss off. Trying to figure out why no one in the movies wears seat belts."

April's immaculate living room was AC chilled. The furnishings are sparse and expensive. Besides the couch and work area, the left, south wall consisted of pale pine bookshelves containing non-fiction books, manufacturers' manuals, and white papers. Molly took the leather office chair at April's long work table where there was a triangle of shade from the glaring windows. She laid out the cash and plastic from the last two days' work.

"The seven hundred?" Molly nudged gently.

"Got the how. Working traces on the who." She rose from the couch and walked naked to the windows, sleep mask up on her bald head. "It wasn't government, the markers were all wrong for that," she spoke to the waves a hundred yards off the white beach.

"Got a suspect?"

"Other than someone we've really torqued, no idea."

"That's quite a list."

"I'll figure it out. It'll take some time. Molly? Look at us. You're a lush, and now I'm a killer. Two twenty-nine-year-old messes."

"Not so. Let's go with endearing lunatics."

April turned and smiled, appreciating that.

"How's the wrist?" she asked.

"Same. Makes me endearingly awkward. Had time to start in on our ransom *clients*?"

"Two, yes. Still mining their files, but I've got enough to send one of them the first message."

"When's Clance gonna arrive?"

"Should've been here yesterday."

"How much did we borrow for the robbery cars? Have to cut him a check."

"I'll give him another ring. After a nap."

Molly took the newspaper from the back of her shorts and laid it out open beside the cash and credit cards. "If you didn't see it online, that Polly's Market *Rambo* was in a vest. He'll be fine. His shot murdered an Icee machine."

"Really?" April turned from the view. She released a full breath.

"Really. I suggest you go do your church thing. Enjoy, work out. Then get back to work."

"Think I will. What are you going to do with your evening?"

"Go hang out at the Oceanside bar."

"Careful, sis. No DUIs and the like."

"Right. I'll behave. Now go pray or whatever it is you do."

April crossed to her bedroom where she fired up her body paint rig and applied a caramel color with sunblock in the mixture. She pulled on a white one-piece Speedo and white ball cap and went downstairs where she kept her stash of surfboards in the screened veranda.

Ten minutes later, she was paddling out into the warm, small waves. The tide was low, and the surf was languid, and she surfed by herself, twenty-five yards from the boys who were better than her. Each wave allowed for a slight drop and a few turns before closing out. She began the cycle of riding and paddling back out, her thoughts cleansed with each lap. Not once did the concerns of the past days intrude while stroking into one fine four-foot blue wave after another.

―――――

An hour and a half later, she sat on the sand beside her board with the orange light of the sunset on her shoulders. She took a deep breath of the bit of surf wax she had brought along and closed her lovely eyes to the deliriously timeless, wonderful scent of coconut.

"Hey, God, how's your day?" she whispered into the warm and humid air. "All is good here. Hope you're enjoying my story. That's why I'm here, right?"

She opened her eyes to watch a handful of white sand granules fall through her cupped fingers, forming a cone mountain between her raised knees.

"Bet you're too busy with your tennis ratchet, smacking asteroids out of our path to watch my movie." She studied the sugary rising pyramid.

She recalled her sixth wave and saw and rode it a second time. After her bottom turn, she leveled off on the translucent wave face and saw a school of white fish running along the white sand bottom. A few inches before the nose of her surfboard, the pack of fish made a flick turn as one and darted for a bit of food or to escape a threat. Seeing their life and drama in the clear window of seawater was many of the delights of her time in surf church. She allowed a smile to play in her lovely thin lips before shaking her head.

"I'm sitting here getting sand in my ass when I've got work to do. Before I go, can you give me a clue about who's angry enough *and* has the resources?"

Standing and brushing sand off her fine peach-shaped rear, she looked to the surf for the last time that day.

"Sorry, sir, I'm gonna take the sharp turn onto Revenge Boulevard."

CHAPTER ELEVEN

Ding Dong

Arriving at midnight, Daytona Beach International Airport didn't have even a slight vibe of its appended "International." Besides his Hawaiian-dressed fellow travelers, all Rick Ables, Jr. saw was work-stunned janitors and shuttered cheap shops washed out in the green-white morgue fluorescent lighting. He took a shuttle to a cheaper off-site car rental lot, wanting to splurge on a fine room at the Hilton. Instead, he settled for a tropical painted room in a forty-six-dollars-per-night shoebox motel, two blocks west of the beach and tourists and boardwalk. As he drove to it, he groused, "Disneyland for adults."

Just up the street, he ate two greasy burgers, staring down the oily French fries and sleeping that off with a three-hour nap. Opening his laptop, he fought and swore at the 'extra charge' slow and hiccupping internet connection.

At six that same morning, he left the motel for breakfast

at a Waffle House. He *dined* at a table against the back wall—a syrup-drenched waffle and a side of hash browns smothered in sausage gravy and two cups of stale, weak coffee.

His next stop was for cooler clothing—a pair of long floral shorts, and a green cotton shirt with a parrot on the breast pocket at a place offering '10,000 T-shirts' and '3 Ts for $10.' Leaving the shop, the heat was stupefying and sticky humid, and he was in a full-body sweat between the door and his beater of a rental car. The AC in the Ford Focus worked well, never mind the fluttering spin of damaged fan blades.

He drove the strip. There were palm trees in sidewalk planters and ridiculously happy-looking tourists walking in packs. It seemed that every other business was a cinderblock and glass nest for real estate buzzards. The one he chose was on the outskirts of Daytona, Ocean View Realty, offering vacation rentals and condos for sale. He liked this one because it was in between a suspect bar called 'The Dicks' and a soon-to-be foreclosed-looking vapor and tattoo shop.

Ignoring the two eager sales agents amidst the other empty desks, he went for the throat of the better-resourced broker, Brenda Glaise, seated in a rear cubicle of the thin and tired decorated office. He planned to strong-arm the real estate broker by flashing his invalid US Marshal's badge. Instead, he decided to smooth talk rather than threaten and frighten.

Brenda Glaise was a plump, tan-baked glossy blonde in a tropically festive blouse with her gold name tag riding the waves of her significant breast. Within three minutes, he had her in a lather by including her in his confidential and vital fugitive search. Same gambit as in Michigan, just a different source for a property and title search with Danser in the Owner Name field.

Unfortunately, Brenda Glaise didn't know how to navigate the database for Owner Name, so she began feeding her noisy, struggling laser printer. Gladly printing off a mound of records, she gave him all the pages of transactions for the past five years in Volusia County, which included Daytona Beach and outlying areas, Ormond-by-the-Sea southward through to the town of Edgewater.

He left with the ream-size printouts with a promise to keep Brenda apprised of the investigation, mentioning that she had already met the federal requirements for a signed commendation.

Deciding to find a new place to hole up, he drove north of Daytona on A1A, finding a cheap motel of row cabins, no swimming pool, and an extra $11.99 per week for wireless internet. Dumping the stack of data on the sticky round table in his room, he went out for an early lunch up the road at some bad greasy-food roadside tavern called Lagerheads, eating in the back of the outdoor area of picnic tables. The décor was beer signs and hanging fishing nets, wood seagulls on the on walls, and sun and stained rough deck flooring. A mixed bag of customers included delighted snowbirds and tourists and bored and hopeless locals.

He shared his lunch with a free cheesy tourist map of Volusia, getting his bearings as light traffic on A1A streamed past twenty feet from the pole and boat rope entrance.

Back inside his dismal and small motel room, the AC was cranked to high offering a chilled mist from the vents. He drank glass after glass of tap water to rinse down the salt of the meal while wading into the four-inch stack of property title change records.

———

It was dark out when he sat down in the rusted steel, orange porch chair outside his door, under a moth-flicked exposed bulb. In his hands were the three pages of details on the Danser residence purchased three years prior.

"Time for a look-see."

The parcel map confused him. Their purchase was of adjoining lots, one zoned residential and the second commercial. The property stretched from something called the Halifax all the way to the sea. The business was constructed in 1961 and the residence in 1996. Referencing the tourist map, he drove north up the two-lane highway, the moon-washed surf to his right and miles of low brush to the left.

Referencing both the parcel and tourist maps while driving, he turned onto Windswept Road. Two hundred yards along, he steered into the sandy driveway, headlights warming the chain protecting the driveway. The top view parcel illustration didn't show the driveway or any connection between the two structures. He sat staring, fingers drumming the steering wheel, the use of a combination lock on the chain speaking loud and clear.

Climbing out in the night, the air sticky with the smell of brackish water, he found a brick-sized rock and threw it. Sensors lit up along the sandy road running inland a quarter mile through vicious vegetation that looked like hundreds of raised sword blades, the shapes of the clustered plants reminding him of sharp pineapple heads.

When the sensors shut off, he got back in the car and drove a hundred yards further west on Windswept Road, parking in the sand to the side.

"Return in the morning? Liking the idea of a daytime, well-armed 'ding dong,'" he said.

He waited for a reply.

His Holy Ghost slid a ballot in front of him, two choices, no suggestion.

Taking up the imagined chad punch pen, he waited for a

hint. A minute later, he was still on his lonesome with this choice.

"Go in under darkness, bypassing the driveway sensors? Brave the razor brush in the dark?"

He waited, alone in the curtained voting booth in his mind.

Impatience and impulse won the night.

At the rear of the rental, he used the trunk light to ponder the luggage one last time before shouldering his pouch with gun and ammo and break-in tools.

The cruel palmetto scratching his hips and elbows, he was twenty yards in when his shoe splashed into muck water, and he sank to one knee. Birds and critters stirred from both sides, and a single word of fear crossed his lips.

"Alligators?"

Climbing out, he backtracked and circled the pond or stream or whatever. Walking the up and down terrain, he continued in a northern direction to the center of the property, his arms and thighs jabbed by the clustered palmettos.

"Please show me a trail connecting the two." He paused and looked skyward.

His cell phone rang and lit up, startling the night. He struggled to pull it from his pants pocket, nearly dropping it when his wrist was gouged by the needle of a thorn branch.

He scrolled through the stream of flagged, unencrypted numerics and interpreted. "Assets transferred offshore."

"They got to the funds?" he asked the black night sky.

Unfrozen? And moved offshore in the blink of a nanosecond. His vengeful reward of their monies vaporizing like a Florida snowball.

Turning around 360 degrees in a slow rotation, fresh sweat broke out up and down his body and flushed his face. Eyes not seeing the stars like tiny diamonds in the black sky, he looked instead for some visage of his holy guide.

"So, so much more than capture." His thoughts flamed in a blinding rage. He received a red-tinged visage of the sisters in tattered and filthy prison jumpsuits, violated repeatedly, impoverished, and ruined. Taking a deep breath, he held it in hoping it would help.

Empowered by his understanding of *Ruach Hakodesh*, the Hole Breath, he trudged forward, weaving the dangerous vegetation, his shoes finding the way as if on their own.

He stumbled and caught himself but not before a razor stalk sliced his thigh.

"I'm coming for you, Fuck One and Fuck Two."

Turning on his phone's flashlight, it appeared that an east-to-west path lay ten yards further. His thoughts had started to wander to the cold morning of his self-baptism and his exorcism of his past life. He shook it off. Five strides further on, his shoe sank to the knee. He splashed into a muck stream of saltwater.

A gray heron took flight from a shoulder-high nest in thrush branches, a prehistoric size bird with a five-foot wing-span alighting at his left arm. Spooked, he spun and fell, face first, arms cartwheeling, right into the blades of palmetto stalks. He screamed and clambered and rolled off onto the sandy soil. His face, neck, and arms were cut deep and scraped and bleeding.

Kneeling in the darkness, he ripped off his new parrot shirt and pressed it against his jaw and cheek to stem the worse of the flow. Sliced deep and stabbed, he raised his right knee and tore off a sleeve to wind around it. Blood dripping from deep wounds in too many places, he tore the shirt into three more pieces and struggled in the darkness to stanch the worst of the injuries.

Rising to his feet, his hands were slippery and bloody.

Standing in his torn and ripped pants, he struggled through the relentless sharp foliage, getting nicked and cut until he was out on the east-to-west narrow path of crunchy sand.

Looking first to the right and then to his left, his vote was still undecided.

"The commercial building or the residence?" He looked into the darkness in both directions.

A familiar, gruff voice spoke from the rear of his thoughts. "Or?"

CHAPTER TWELVE

Fly on the Cake

At ten o'clock the next night, Molly entered April's place by the back door and climbed the stairs to the living room. Not having heard the loud Vespa, April turned around from her array of monitors.

"You walked?" she asked.

"Yea, I couldn't find the keys."

"Get you something to eat?"

"Had a thought," Molly drank from her thermos. "But I lost it on the walk."

"You working tonight?"

"Nope, well maybe some. Heading over to the Oceanside. Borrow your car?"

"Sure. Keys in the bowl."

"Thinkin' I'll have a Jo night."

"Tell her hello."

Molly went to the kitchen and cracked an ice cube tray

and stirred through the liquor bottles for the green glass of Tanqueray. She left for the start of the night with her bartender gal pal, Jo, a willing accomplice.

She gave April one of her rehearsed, dazzling, heartbreaking smiles. She wore a red-mahogany wig and green hazel eyes.

April went back to work. She wrapped up establishing their new offshore account, seeing the confirmation of the account's activation.

Next on the list was the new ransom clients while she waited for the professor's status on her side tray laptop. Having decided to try a shot-gun style, she copy and pasted and sent off the two ransom notes, one to a cosmetic surgeon in Orlando and the other to a DUI attorney in San Diego. Both were exhaustively researched and their personal mail and files rifled and swiped.

The sensors woke up the computer monitor at her left side, bringing up the camera arrays. April studied each, even though only one feed had a red pulsing indicator. That was camera eleven, the gate cam. A car was idling at the chained driveway entrance. She watched on until the small car backed out onto Windswept Road and drove off to scenic A1A,

"Neckers or lost tourists." She turned back to her next task.

Into the wee hours of the night, she researched three new marks, sitting in the warm monitor glow.

At four in the morning, there was the uniquely assigned sparrow chirp alert from the side tray laptop.

Using his magical coding, the community college professor had massaged encrypted certificates and certifications to unfreeze and transfer the seven hundred thousand under the guise of a Bolivian banking officer with federal authority.

She had a contract with her off-and-on partner in electronic crime, Jeff. With kiddies and an ex-wife and house payments in arrears, he had more than earned the $21,000 for nineteen hours of work.

She read his succinct and oh-so-Jeff closing, "Done."

"Ta-da." She swiveled in her chair, bare feet dancing on the flooring.

She sent a text.

April: *Thank you. Brilliant. I'll wire you after the funds land in the new account.*

Her smile tightening away, her lovely eyes narrowed as she typed a second message to Jeff the Prof.

April: *Give you anther three percent if you can get me the "who.'*

If the culprit was the authorities, there was nothing to do. If the thief was some clever and disgruntled victim, he or she needed to be boot-squashed like a fat cockroach.

She spent twenty minutes counting assets currently in hand, the seven hundred not available for twenty-four hours. Prior cash and Molly's cocktail party take was eleven grand minus what they owed Clance for the strip mall cars.

There was also the stolen credit card numbers and skimmer proceeds to max out for cash through her anonymous Birmingham contact, coming with a thirty percent fee.

Calling an end of the night shift as five in the morning rolled around, April shut down the computers and swiveled to the big windows, still dark, no glow of dawn.

"Sleep, oh, creamy warm sleep, I'm on my way."

———

Molly took the stairs to the rooftop bar at Oceanside where her bartender pal, Jo, greeted her.

"Hi, love, who are you?"

"Darcy, the redheaded tourist." Molly had memorized the first name on the new driver's license.

"Well, climb aboard, Miss Darcy."

"How's my Jo?"

"Dazzling, bored, and thirsty. You?"

"Same except for the *bored*."

The row of bar stools along the dark wood countertop was full, a line-up of couples and solo drinkers, all yakking and laughing. She took the spare at the end by the wall and kitchen elevator. Beyond the bar, late-night diners were enjoying the view of silver waves breaking on the low- tide sands.

"Got the look right," Jo said.

Molly was in ridiculously white sailor pants and a baby blue tank top loose enough for the allure of the curves of her firm breasts to show at both sides. She was wearing entirely too much shiny gold jewelry and carried a floral clutch.

"Was going for southern cougar," she told Jo.

"Nailed it, except you're too young."

Jo's blonde hair reminded Molly of her sister's *JF* wig. She was five-foot-ten-inches tall and slender and had quick, curious eyes and a constant beautiful smile. Molly watched Jo chat up customers and pour drinks, all quick and fluid efforts, and thought again—*Jo's a fast and nimble low-slung Mustang with tinted windows.*

"What're you drinking?" Jo called down the bar.

"*We* are drinking tonics and Tanqueray."

Jo poured two over chip ice, set one by the cash register and the other before Molly.

Fifteen minutes in, a drink she hadn't ordered was set down beside her hand. Something from a blender and lime-colored with a wedge of pineapple, and thankfully, no umbrella.

Molly didn't look. That could wait. She took a sip, puckered, and pushed the drink forward. Sure enough, a male shoulder appeared at her side two minutes later, saying, "Not to your taste? Like something else?"

"Don't do kiddie drinks. Darcy. You?"

He told her his name and leaned in, no stool available.

"Vacation?" he asked.

"Escape."

He turned, and when he caught Jo's eye, called along, "Two more of whatever Miss Darcy is enjoying."

"Thanks. Why are you here?"

His pause said, "huh?" He found his footing quickly, saying, "Work-cation."

"Two types of bartenders..." he went on, out of who knew where, "... the philosophical and alcoholic."

She let that just float out there until it dissolved.

They yakked and bantered until he realized he was striking out. She rolled his card before he wandered off, taking a glance into the crowd along the bar, offering her sultry eyes and secretive smile.

Her second mark was in a polo shirt and had the look of a local real estate agent—tan, a nearly handsome face, and a wedding ring shadow. They shared a single round and a card flip before Molly got rid of him by going off for the restroom and counting slowly to seventy.

There was no action for the next half hour. She waited patiently, watching the tourists and local bumblers with blurred eyes raised to the sports on the bar television when not sneaking takes on Molly's almost spilling breasts.

She took to chatting with Jo after moving to a vacated

stool near the center of the bar. The crowd was thinning as the night wore on. A married couple to her left began talking her up, asking questions about 'fun things to do.' She offered trite suggestions and rolled the hubby's American Express card after he placed it on top of hers.

The night played out, a pleasant blur of tropical music and late-night voices, the air cozy warm, another perfect Florida night. The dining area emptied except for the table candles wavering in the gentle breeze.

Not trusting her liquor-slowed hand, she left the open purse to her right alone and let the woman return from a pee and makeup break with her monies intact. A man sat down beside her to the right. He was wearing cargo shorts, expensive loafers, and a festive bowling shirt. He was using cash, so they chatted briefly before she moved on.

Between the time she first climbed the stairs until Jo closed the bar at two in the morning, she had a decent take and a heady buzz going. Her efforts to control the throttle of her alcohol intake had failed. It had helped to be ordering for both herself and Jo as her gal pal was more of a sipper.

They took Jo's mustard-colored Jeep into Daytona to the upscale 509 Club. All cool blue neon lighting and a good-size crowd in the crystal everything décor.

The two were asked to join a party in the VIP lounge where Molly flipped two cards while Jo entertained with salty tales of bartender adventures.

A hazy invite came the girls' way from a couple of guys in starched and pressed casual clothing. They and Jo had just snorted something, Molly declining the straw.

The four of them took a warm night stroll from the 509 to a biker bar on Main Street, the building looking like a former small-town bank. The two men found a table, and Molly excused herself for the restroom where she stood at the sink and scribbled down the credit card details from earlier in the night on a pad inside her clutch.

She returned to the others seated at a table crowded with shot glasses of mind-twisting tequila and a silver pail of boiled peanuts. A half hour later, the girls and their Canadian sunbirds were on the road to the guys' big boat in a harbor slip, Jo driving, following their large rental car.

The foursome navigated the dock walks of the Daytona Marina to a good-size powerboat gangway, the men offering beefy hands to the two beautiful women's elbows, guiding them aboard.

The interior of the twenty-eight-foot boat said fishing adventure rental. It also said to Molly, "Good for wife avoidance and heavy drinking." The salon and galley were in dimmed amber lighting, and syrupy 80s pop music played from the helm speakers.

The Canadian brothers in crime looked pleased with themselves and their surroundings, especially with two intoxicated twenty-something lovelies. Molly was still focused enough to note where wallets and keys were casually dropped as Jo gushed in delight with the boat, asking them about its operation and the kind of fish they were after, winking in a blink to Molly.

Fuzzy time passed with drinks and moves about the boat, four voices warbling in laughter and loud inanities.

Just before sunrise, Molly stood in the salon bathroom with her hand inside the shower, testing and adjusting the water temperature. One of the Canadians stood at her side, shirt off, revealing his farmer's tan, making slurred and lurid suggestions. Molly's final liquid vignette was possibly of her pulling off her pale blue tank top. She wasn't sure.

CHAPTER THIRTEEN

Justice: The Sequel

Rick Ables, Jr. woke up sharing his pillow with a bloody wash-cloth, the bedding over his naked body splotched with blood-stains. Rolling carefully onto his side, he dry-swallowed two pain pills and one of the antibiotics from the ER pharmacy the night before. He had forcefully waved the two nurses and doctor from his many slashes and deep cuts, making them focus only on the five-inch gash on his cheek and jaw.

He pressed his tongue to the inside of his sutured cheek. The night before he had been able to poke his tongue clean through the five-inch gash. The sheets were stuck to his wounds with crimson dried blood. He pulled them away and swung his legs around and stood. Glaring across the tiny motel room at the dusty television, he ran through his shopping list again. A second run-through, and it was memorized.

Locating his shoes, he pulled on a clean shirt and pants from his suitcase. He found his wallet and keys in the pockets of his tattered and stained pants from the night before. He left to drive south into Daytona for some shopping.

With a plastic shopping basket in hand, he worked the aisles of the CVS under strong white lighting and nearly frigid AC. He grabbed a throwaway razor, sewing kit, hand mirror, bandages, medical tape, and ointments.

The sales clerk gratefully ignored his stitched and ruined face, the row of quarter-inch sutures looking like a leaning ladder. She focused on scanning and ringing him up, taking the cash from his blood-crusted fingers without comment.

Back inside his beach-cabin room with his shopping bag on the bloodied bed, he undressed for a shower to cleanse before starting his wound sewing. Chewing two more bitter pain pills, he stepped inside the warm streaming water, rotating and rubbing his hands. Clumps of fresh and dried blood dropped forming a red and purple drain swirl at his bare feet.

Patting his skin dry with the last clean towel, he ignored the mirror for the time being.

There was a knock on the door.

"Housecleaning."

"Sheets and towels," he called back.

Sitting at the round table, he used the hand mirror to shave his left ruined cheek and jaw liking how turning his head said, *ugly but clean-shaven on one side, but drop-dead handsome on the other*. He grinned in admiration of his divided face and went to work with needle and thread on the deep jagged cuts on his knee, forearms, shoulder, and thigh. He ignored his clipped left ear liking its new edgy, pointed look.

An hour later, he lay down on the bed and pulled the ruined bedding up over the length of his body and tossed the bloody washcloth on his pillow to the floor.

Taking his cell phone off the nightstand beside his pill bottles, he skimmed the internet news from Michigan. There were no videos, but he found three brief articles about the unfortunate houseboat fire and death.

His revised plans came into slow focus, a film in grainy black and white. Closing his eyes, he asked his holy ghost for inspiration. Coloration and theme music rose and stitched together the flow of steps to permanently shut down Gash One and Gash Two. The movie, an inspired vision, came into crisp cinematic clarity. With a blink of a memory of his brother's flaming death, a new ending came to him from above.

They had rotated the table on him, and now it was his time to spin it back around. There would be no attempts to smoke them out for capture. Instead, he watched a pyre roar into flaming life as he walked away in a manful, satisfied style. He heard the beloved home crash down into itself under black billowing smoke and climbing flames.

The spirit laid out nearly all the puzzle pieces for him to put into place.

"More shopping to do." He opened his eyes.

Using a motel pad and pen, he made a list. That done, he reclined back and closed his eyes again. The movie needed one more addition.

Eating two more pain pills, he rewound and watched the movie play through to the ending on the theater screen in his head. He waited for guidance as the credits scrolled down the screen, his name appearing often. The movie title came to his groggy mind and appeared, the lettering bold and edgy.

Justice: The Sequel

He thanked his inspired ghost.

CHAPTER FOURTEEN

Strange Things

April bicycled over to Klave's on her fat-tired beach cruiser, the late morning sky a peerless blue and the air sticky and hot. After waving to David Klave and the guys, she took the stairs to the loft on the third floor.

She found Molly on her planked kitchen floor, covered with a spare-room blanket and head on a couch pillow. Before her was the contents of two stolen wallets spilled out beside a soggy note pad of scribbled credit card details.

"Jo drive you home?" she asked softly.

"No idea."

"You all right?"

"Woke up in a strange place with a strange person having done strange things."

"Again."

"Fucking ditto. Espresso, please."

April left her there and brewed a pot and took down two cups.

Molly sat up slowly, closing her eyes.

"April, I've made a choice. A decision."

"Share?"

"Go downstairs and get Dennis. He'll drive me."

"*That* decision? Oh, you're a darling, smart one."

Gathering up the wallets and note pages to take home for processing, April slid them in her wide summer smock pocket and went downstairs and to the front of the boat repair and storage shop.

"Molly's gonna borrow Dennis for his lunch break," she told David Klave, leaning in his office door. "I think she might finally be done."

"About time. Good."

He pointed to a trailered twenty-four-foot party and fishing boat.

"He's got a manifold replacement going."

April climbed the rolling ladder beside the boat, finding Dennis down in the engine hold, an array of tools laid out at the ready on the fiberglass deck at his shoulder.

"Molly's going to lunch with you, kay?"

"Sure," Dennis smiled up from the hold. "Let me get this last bolt, and we're outta here."

Fifteen minutes later, Molly climbed inside Dennis's battered, but smooth-running family minivan. She swept the seat free of fast-food wrappers and energy drink cans.

"Not a single pithy peep out of you," she said.

"Got it. Drive with it zipped."

They rolled north into town on John Anderson Road paralleling the river. At the turn onto El Granada, Molly looked the strip malls over.

"Hit the liquor store?" she asked.

"Not even if you're holding my hand, cutie."

"Use *cutie* again, and I'll bash you with my cast."

"Loud and clear. Liking the idea of a different life?"

"Swap some parts, yes."

They crossed over the El Granada Bridge, the Halifax running wide and royal blue below. A half mile up the other side of the river, Dennis took a left, and they entered residential back streets. Most of the lawns and driveways of the flat-roof homes were littered with boy toys—trailered fishing skiffs, jet skis, kayaks, and jeeps under repair. The curbs were stacked high with Hurricane Mathew debris.

The row of stop signs led to a gray stone church of unimposing size. A lawn marque had that week's inspirational message.

'*What Happens in Vegas is Forgiven Here*'

Parking in the back among a half dozen cars, Dennis circled the minivan and got Molly's door for her.

"Doing okay?" he asked.

"Cloudy and shaky with a forty-percent chance of rain."

"In hell? Twist of guts and thoughts?"

Molly nodded, tears welling.

"Good because it can be the last time you're there."

Following Dennis through a maze of church hallways and doors, Molly smelled burned coffee and ignored the fliers taped to the walls. They came to an open door of a well-lit conference room painted childish yellows and green and warm pink.

"Hello, sweetie and welcome, you're in the right place," a kind woman at the door said.

On the sidewall was a poster with the Twelve Steps

written on ladder rungs.

Shaking, sweating, and thirsty, Molly stepped inside, being offered a smile and the hand from a woman with a face like a dried apple, skin the color of wheat dough.

Molly looked around the square table of a dozen or so tired, but mostly happy faces.

"I'm confused, is this Kiwanis?" she quipped.

"Sense of humor will serve you well. Grab a donut or a coffee and one of the better chairs."

Dennis pointed to two free chairs at the square table of eleven attendees, opposite four more crab-apple faces to the right. To Molly's left sat two thugs with neck tattoos and crumbled signature sheets, one of them glaring at her, the other fascinated with a coffee stir stick.

After the reading of several suggestions from a page in a plastic sleeve, they went around the table, each introducing themselves. Molly adopted the format of the others.

"I'm Molly. I'm a motorcycle racer... and alcoholic."

"Welcome, love, only the last part matters."

A smiling, handsome young man with clear eyes spoke next.

"Accept whatcha can't change, change what you can, be smart enough to know the difference."

"Back in the good days..." one of the elderly grouches interrupted, "... we took off the baby gloves and fought the bottle with our fists. Should be more of that."

"Pay him no mind. He's trudging the road to happy misery," Dennis whispered.

"You're in the best place on the planet to get the hooch outta your life," someone chimed in.

"We simply describe what it was like, what landed us here, and what's going on now," another voice explained.

The first hand up was to Molly's right. An attractive, fashionably dressed and coifed Asian woman in her forties told a horrifying story of humiliation and scars, followed by a sketch of calm and easy but busy clean days.

Most of the other eleven spoke, telling their story, except the thug with his coffee stick.

The kindly woman who had greeted Molly looked along the row of faces to her.

"When I came in, I had a head full of clowns, midgets, and firetrucks," the woman said. "I was lost in the heebie-jeebies and just starting my detox spastics."

Turning to Molly, she added, "All ya gotta do is ride out the shakes and start enjoying life again. This ain't brain surgery."

Molly took Dennis's hand for a squeeze of warmth.

The last to speak was a sheriff on leave who was headed for a review board to possibly get his badge, his career, and his life back.

"I derailed over a number of years, a slow but killer train wreck. Now I've got some of the pieces back and the engine fired. Still have a lot of shoveling to do to get my wife back, but I'm up to it. We're *all* up to it if we choose."

Molly grabbed onto the train-crash metaphor and played with from many angles. Seeing how it fit, she raised her hand.

"I'm in."

———

When Molly left with Dennis, April biked back to her home. Before heading off for some waves, she went through her messages. There was only one that caught her full attention. It was from Jeff the Prof.

Got in as your bank's COI. The fingerprints on the freeze resemble a govt job, but the lack of legal tentacles says a connected but single source. My bet? It's someone you or your sister twisted and broke.

Frowning at the monitor, she thought back through the flicking memories of faces and thefts. There were many very pissed-off clients and victims. Just the number of them got her thinking of taking a long nap to sweep away the countless possible threats. Before heading off to her bed, she replied.

Thank you. Please continue working it. I want a name. Pay rate the usual.

Tempted to open one of her favorite Highsmith novels, April instead crawled to the middle of her big bed and nested with her knees drawn up under layers of sheets and blankets. As always, to rinse away her worries, she visualized the curves of glassy waves, each one rising and smoothly folding over, offering her a canvas of clear water to surf.

Sometime later, Molly climbed into the bed and nuzzled up close to her back.

"Hi, ya." April stirred, half surfacing from a dreamy sleep.

"I know. I need a shower," Molly whispered. "I'm sweating like a third striker."

April felt the quaking in her sister's fingertips on her shoulder.

"I'll get up. Make you something to eat," April said.

"Thank you. Sugar on everything, please."

April returned with sliced peaches and grapes sprinkled with powdered sugar and a glass of chocolate milk.

"Had a thought." Molly chewed a peach wedge. "There was all this babble about God. Sure, he's a great guy, but what about Satan? He's always on stage, on the other shoulder, whispering and seductive, working his own game in our heads."

"Okay..."

"So here we are going through our lives with one voice on each side."

She paused to sip chocolate milk from the straw.

"Like two well-dressed chipmunks, one white and the other red," Molly added.

"Faith based on childhood cartoons, I'm liking it," April encouraged.

"You?"

"It's not thought through, but I'm leaning toward the God question as being too deep for my wee brain. All I need is a run of good choices. Better decisions. I've come up with exactly one."

"Which is?"

"No more guns. No matter what we get ourselves into."

"Hmm, gotta think on that. I'm gonna sleep now. Gotta do the detox thing."

April left her sister and changed into her Speedo and surf cap. She walked the warm sand to the beach for a handful of late afternoon waves. After a snack, she followed the call of her computers.

Launching a TOR session, she worked on the ransoms. There were new marks to research and hack, going for embarrassing and/or criminal emails, messages, photos, and files. From the current list of nine candidates, three were possible *clients*, each with a documented trail of very bad choices and acts, all variations of the usual greed and lust and vanity and illegal shenanigans.

Two hours in, she took a break and called Clance again. She left another voicemail and followed that with a text:

. . .

April: *Hey ya, you're pushing this bugger off thing too far. All's okay? I miss you.*

While staring at her cell phone and waiting, her thoughts returned to the likely suspect of the banking freeze. Her and Molly's past was littered with men and women burned hard. Clance's older brother came to mind—*Jr.* She smirked, recalling how that always got his hackles up when Clance called him that. Like so many, she and Molly had spun, washed, and dried him hard, but he was government—a marshal—and not what Professor Jeff was seeing.

As the sunlight faded in the big windows across the room, she worked the ransom negotiations with the current clients, thinking each next step through slowly before firing off replies that cranked up the heat and threats. She included ugly descriptions of the nasty fallout should they decide not to play along.

Back to digging up evidence of wrongdoings and embarrassing moral decisions on the new clients, she worked past midnight. While shutting down her computers for the night, she checked her cell phone again for a reply from Clance. Seeing none and frowning, she left her workspace, willing him to knock it off and message her.

With Molly shaking and sleeping in her bed, April took to the front room couch to read a few chapters into one of the Ripley books. Laying it aside on the coffee table, she pulled the wondrous thick blankets up around her head for slumber. Molly's question of 'good and bad' and the two voices played briefly in her twilight thoughts. Rolling over, she brought up the first memory of a smooth and clean wave forming. Within minutes, she was gliding downward through layers of unconsciousness, warm-water surf guiding her along.

CHAPTER FIFTEEN

White Lilies

In his bathroom, Rick Ables, Jr. mixed Neosporin and scar cream in a paper cup beside the one-pot coffee maker. Sitting on the foot of his bed, he finger-dabbed the goo on his many wounds. Wiping his oily fingers on the bedding, he tore his shopping list off the pad on the desk and left.

The rental car was a steam box. Blinking away the sweat from his eyes, he started it up. As the air chilled, the vents streamed something that smelled like carpet cleaner. Heading north, the razor scrub brush and seagrass along the sides of the road gave way to towering condos and hotels, each the color of children's play chalk.

Entering Daytona Beach, the traffic slowed along the strip. The sidewalks were lined with palm trees and tourists in lousy loud shirts gawking at arcade and fast-food doorways. He studied them, frowning, their heads rotating like sun-cooked iguanas in bad hats. Two traffic lights in, the *blat, blat,*

blat of three low and fat Harleys pulled alongside—all black, chrome, and orange. The riders all looked like hardened, long-term criminals. When they turned in on a side street, he changed lanes and followed.

One block in, he had found biker's row. Along both sides of the street, bikes were parked rear tire in. Their owners were milling about the sidewalks and bar entrances, the men in beards and cheap sunglasses, their women in low-cut t-shirts, all cleavage, peroxide hair, and leather. He rolled past the Boot Hill Saloon, the Full Moon, and the Iron Horse with outdoor tables full of bikers drinking at picnic tables. He drove in deeper, past the tourist bikers with polished chrome and expensive paint jobs on their rides, passing the Metal Pig and The Losers Saloon. Parking in a brick alley, he hoofed out to the crowded sidewalk, standing under the awning of the Hot Leather shop, seeing what he wanted across the road, a narrow shop, Spike's Tats.

Inside the converted barbershop, he walked past a couple in their fifties, both in black clothing, not mindful of the heat. They were flipping through a tattoo catalog at the counter. The owner was seated in the shadows at the back, taking a break beside a gurgling espresso machine on an inks and needles table.

The tall, fit man looked up at Rick Ables, Jr. slowly. He was brutally handsome and clear-eyed sober and spoke in a gravelly voice.

"Help you, son?" The 'son' was interesting—the two of them were about the same age.

"I'll wait," Rick replied, gesturing to the couple at his back.

"Long as you like. Have a seat." He nodded to the barber chairs before the row of mirrors and went back to finger skimming a worn blue paperback.

Rick stayed on his feet, pretending interest in the

photographs of fresh tattoos taped to the mirrors and pinned to the walls.

The couple left with a "thanks" and "we'll be back," and the man dog-eared the book and set it aside.

"Name's Marty. How can I help you?"

Rick flashed his badge, and Marty rolled his eyes slowly, looking both bored and displeased.

"I'm looking to buy a couple of throw-aways," Rick said.

"Wrong place for it. Care for an espresso?" Marty turned and placed two tiny cups on the counter in matching little saucers.

"Know a guy?" Rick shook his head at the offer of a coffee.

"If you'll leave without disturbing my customers, I can give you a number."

"A number will do."

Marty wrote smoothly on a Post-it and held it out. Rick pocketed it.

"Doesn't come back to me." Marty's voice was solid and dismissive. He busied himself with a box of sugar cubes and a little silver spoon.

"No, it won't." Rick left.

———

He made the call from the rental car and drove back out onto the strip and south, deeper inside the carnival-like run of sea-view restaurants, beachwear stores, and hotel entrances. A mile in, he parked in an eight-dollar-a-day sandlot, the skyline a colorful painting of metal works elevating roller-coaster tracks. Shrieks of frightened laugher and rumbling fast steel wheels filled the hot air as he crossed the street and entered the boardwalk, passing the entrance to a clam-shell open-air pavilion.

Walking through the crowd of vacant-eyed teenagers, gawking fat tourists, and old people on their last legs, he ignored the occasional fearful eyes taking in the ruined side of his face. For the overfed children with runny noses and food smeared on their mouths, he gave them a full view, enjoying their fright.

The heat was blazing, his body hot and sweating as he made his way along the boardwalk among the glaring colors and the senseless blasting music. There were walk-ups serving fried snacks and drinks and shops selling beach towels, trinkets, and sunscreen. Passing the first of the arcades, he entered the Coney Dog, weaving through the families hovering over their meals, making his way to the rear along the yellow tables with fish hooks, lures, and bobbers embedded in the clear veneer.

A scrawny guy with nervous, pressed-together beads for eyes was studying him, working the straw in his large soda. He sat with his back to the wall, was unshaven, and wore a grimy apron over a polo shirt dotted with dog heads.

Rick Ables, Jr. sat down across from the creep, resting his arms on the sticky table, sharing the deep cuts and slices on his hands. He opened his windbreaker, letting him see the badge as he took out a fat envelope.

"Nice face, mister poh-lice-man." The guy took in Rick Ables, Jr.'s sliced and red and stitched face, giving his straw another suck, trying to mask a tinge of fear and find his cool.

Rick Ables, Jr. watched on, not saying a word.

"You wanted two..." the man said, "... but you get one for the price of one."

Rick Ables, Jr. removed half the cash from the envelope before sliding it across.

"What you want is in the john under the mop."

Finding the 9mm wrapped in newspaper, Rick Ables, Jr. left the Coney Dog and walked the crowd in the heat, the clickety-clack 70s music from all around giving him a headache.

His next stop was the West Daytona Walmart where he bought a roll of black Gorilla tape, a throwaway backpack, a black long-sleeve shirt, and pants. He also picked up a manual staple gun loaded with half inchers and a reel of quarter-inch twine. Last on his shopping list was a wiring tool kit and a packet of multicolored zip ties.

At Rex's Bow & Rifle, he bought a new 9mm clip and a box of bullets before driving out to Deland to an army surplus warehouse store. He found the right kind of timer fuses and had to smooth the owner in the back of the place in the storeroom. Twenty minutes later, he left with three one-point-two pounds US G.I. military gel fuel packs of diethylene glycol.

His last stop was at a local florist where he purchased two bouquets of white lilies.

Back at his beach cabin, he called the Florida Power Company and canceled the girls' account with immediate shut-off authorized. On the foot of his bed, he had another dabbing session with his special blend of ointments before crawling under the covers for a nap. Closing his eyes with a prayer to the ghost, he offered a plea for surety and guidance. And sweet victory.

He was answered with a vision of the sisters departing some time before, driving off into the sunset, their shared laughter at him haunting and piercing. The memory was painfully fresh and pushed the lever in his head that drew back the stage curtain, allowing the ghost to stroll out on center stage for the first time that night.

"Let them laugh," his partner said. "That way they'll never see it coming."

CHAPTER SIXTEEN

No Shakes and Twitches

Molly woke entangled in her bedding, the blankets twisted around her lower legs and kicked to the foot, the top sheet pulled over her head. She lay perfectly still, and the first thing she saw when she opened her eyes was her wrist in the cast lying in a pool of mid-morning sunlight. Barely daring to breathe, she felt out her physical and mental state. A molasses-like memory played. The night before, the boring and sober night before. A one-eyed glance at her night table said it all—an open can of 7Up instead of a tumbler of gin.

Climbing from the bed, she crossed the loft to her open shower and washed and rinsed in cool water, focusing most of her efforts on her face and shaved head, rubbing at the cobwebs of a foreign sleep in contrast to passing out. Forgoing bra and panties, she got into her black boots and chose a soft silk dress of blue with sun dots. The final touch was her short and black, bowl- cut *Moe* wig.

She took the plank stairs down to the first floor, hearing the voices and machinery of David Klave and his crew hard at work out front. She found Allison at his workbench using tiny tools under his lit magnification lamp, a scatter of electronic bits to the left and a cannibalized race bike carburetor to the right. Molly rested her fingertips on the bench, just to the side of his vision, to announce her presence without startling him.

"A minute," he whispered, his fingers making minute adjustments under the round magnified view.

"You got it."

She turned to the new, unpainted café race bike frame that had come in and stepped over to circle and admire its beautiful, skeletal potential.

As if staying on topic with her, Allison said," The engine came in. I'll get it uncrated later today."

Swiveling around, he took in the lines of Molly's sensual shape inside the sheer dress, the silk clinging to her skin from the heat and humidity.

"Put your eyes back in," she admonished, smiling.

"Never, love. Someday you'll see my light."

"Oh? It's your *light* you want to amuse me with?"

His eyes rose to hers, and they shared a criminal grin.

"No morning thermos?" His gaze studied her calm expression.

"No thermos," was all she allowed. No quip, no sarcasm.

"Proud of you. I've finished five of the new Wi-Fi skimmer models. You working tonight?"

"Yes. Gotta pay the rent."

"And entry fees. The package for the Santa Cruz race came in."

The Santa Cruz 200 was being hosted by one of the few US cities crazy enough to see the sense in holding a street race of café bikes—the overpowered, fat-tired, absurdly loud retro motorcycles.

"I've got a thing to do," Molly said. "Then let's go get April to cut some checks."

"Another lunch date with Dennis the Letch?"

"Yes. When I get back, teach me the grinder on the race frame?"

"Sure. We can also start the engine rebuild. Have a good meeting with Dennis. Watch out for his hands."

"I watch out for everyone's hands. Thank you for the skimmer work. I'm jazzed to see them feeding data."

"Hotel ATMs? Or?"

"Night clubs tonight."

Dennis the Letch called from the front of the building, grease wiping his hands with a rag, looking in through the boats under repair.

"Miss Molly, you game?"

She kissed the top of Allison's head and headed out front.

"I'm in. You're driving today. Keeps your hands and eyes busy." She smiled to Dennis as she started forward through the angled rows of storage boats.

———

April put her surfboard in the rack and stepped into the outdoor shower. She put her white surf cap on a nail and pulled off her white Speedo that gathered around her ankles to rinse. She soaped and washed her tall and lovely and ripe, beautiful figure. Hanging her swimsuit on a peg, she padded naked and bald to her work area and sat, alighting her computers.

The first of her ransom marks was being receptive and nicely frightened, scurrying to pull together the big chunk of money needed to rescue her wonderful life. The other was balking, still feigning confusion with the demand, acting like they didn't understand the threat. In the email from the first, the mark said that the monies were being pulled together, but she wanted a conversation, in other words, a negotiation and plea. April had enough evidence on the shady lawyer's illegal and unethical antics to take her down hard.

"Shovel time." April scooted her chair along her desk and tapped the right-hand computer to life. It opened to a TOR session. It was time to finish researching their third mark. The search of the data dump Jeff the Prof had provided was focused on finding an additional lever.

It took April two hours to follow a quirky and out-of-character email reference from four years prior, which led to a block of files within that time frame of two weeks. She reorganized the mark's files by date stamps and then by type. Four files had numeric gibberish for titles but were appended with .MOV file types. She slid the four over into a new folder before opening the first one.

A QuickTime film opened, and April watched no further in than the professionally produced movie title, *Rich Punished Milf*.

She ran the second film to the slow fade of the title, before closing it. This one was titled *Surprised & Pleasured*.

The third movie was called *Taken*. She shut it off as soon as the opening music began to play.

She let the fourth film, *Taken Two,* play long enough to see her mark's hair-tossed face, her significant ass raised in the middle of a bed with a gym rat behind her in a black G-string.

All four movies were twenty years old.

"Bet she's not going to want that viewed by the press or her courtroom pals." April packaged the four files as attachments in a new email to the 1-800 lawyer and sent it off without comment. It was best to let the mark percolate for a few days before pitching the ransom.

It was easy money if one had the resources, chose the right clients, and was willing to put in the hours and days of shovel work. April could be patient when necessary, focusing on the payout, a small amount from the mark, but significant to her and Molly. She had long ago brushed aside all qualms about what she was doing to lives for profit. This was business, and no lives were ruined unless they went into stupid mode and refused to understand the threat and the amount of damage they risked by trying to talk down the amounts or worse, taking a high-ground stance against the blackmail.

April worked another hour on a fourth mark's research, placing two calls to Jeff the Prof for advice and questions. She took a short break for a glass of milk and a bowl of peach slices. Before leaving the kitchen, she placed another call to Clance and left a worried voicemail.

"Please check in with me, my darling ugly one."

Sometime after six o'clock, she heard Molly's loud Vespa pull into the ease-way between the house and garage. Her sister and Allison entered, chatting and laughing as they went straight to her refrigerator for ice and sodas.

"Get out your checkbook," Molly called, and April pulled her *JF* wig on from the side table to look presentable for Allison as well as her white shorts and t-shirt hanging over the back of her chair.

"What are you two buying?" she called back across the room to the kitchen.

"Entry fees, bike electronics, and half of the *Café Racer* parts catalog."

April rotated her chair around as Molly and Allison sat down on the white couch facing her, a plate set in the space between them. Allison was studying and carefully selecting from the splay of cheese slices and crackers while Molly parked her black boots on the coffee table, showing a rare and refreshed and calm smile.

"Look, no shakes and twitches." Molly held out her hand, the glass of soda steady.

"Makes me very happy," April said.

The property sensors went off, activating a display on April's center monitor.

"Loose dog." She ignored the display of camera angles and took her checkbook out from the top side drawer.

"Who to?" she asked.

Allison read off the company names from a scrap of paper while standing and crossing to April. She laid the paper flat and pressed the creases and wrote the first check, reading the amount in Allison's leisurely elegant handwriting.

She wrote the other two, and he folded and pocketed the three checks.

Seconds later, the power went off.

April whelped and spun around to her worktable. Her computers had gone dark. The Smart UPS battery back-up system kicked in, and the machines started rebooting.

Power to the rest of the house came back on with the grumbled start of a generator. The AC and lights warmed. The generator coughed from underfoot, and the power died for good.

"Where's your genny?" Allison asked.

"Basement. Would you?" April said.

"Of course. Is she fueled?"

"Guess not, dammit."

"On it." Allison left for the cellar door in the short hall to April's bedroom.

CHAPTER SEVENTEEN

The Attack

Rick Ables, Jr. parked in the sand and seagrass alongside A1A in front of April's house and the wood walk to the beach. With his backpack shouldered and the two bouquets in hand, he walked the sand trail far enough to see across the entire front of the structure.

The place had no formal front door, negating his planned fantasy, "*Ding, dong. Hello again.*"

Frustrated, he got back in his car and drove north to Windswept Road and parked in full view of the sensors and cameras at the chained driveway. He walked up the middle of the sand driveway to the east-to-west path marked by knobby tire tracks and footprints and turned to the right.

After a couple of rises and turns, one of the sister's homes came into full view, its pristine white-on-white paint eschewing the candy pastels so common. The garage and house were blasé in design, resembling a middle-class track home dropped on the beach.

He entered the garage by the side door, needing to borrow a ladder. He found one in the shadows, leaning against a double refrigerator size steel box in the back of the two parked vehicles.

Setting the ladder down in the shade of the breezeway between the garage and house, he climbed the back steps, considered knocking for amusement, but instead opened the unlocked door and carried the ladder inside. Resting it against the wall of the short hall, he took out his 9mm. After peeking in on the bathroom and two bedrooms on each side, he walked soft-footed to the kitchen entrance with the living room opening out before him, the big windows filled with an evening view of the beach and ocean.

Seeing the back of a head over the couch back, he looked to April off to the left at a table of computers.

He let the chambering of the gun announce his arrival.

Both heads turned to him, saw the gun, and recognized his face, no matter its damage, and froze. He set the heavy backpack on the kitchen island, and with his other hand, unzipped it and took out the two plastic-wrapped bouquets of white lilies.

"Parting gifts," he said to both, setting the flowers on the island.

The sisters got up slowly and stood shoulder to shoulder at April's work area.

"*Jr.*, how thoughtful. And odd," April said.

His left nostril arched at the 'Jr.'

"Inspired by the ghost. Saw two black caskets with the white flowers on top."

"Still listening to your little friend in the clouds? You're as strange and confused as ever." April dismissed him bravely.

He waved the handgun to April's desk before leveling it on her.

"First thing on the list. Need a check written. Make it out for an even five hundred thousand. Should leave enough for funeral expenses," he said to her.

She got their checkbook and a pen from a desk drawer and wrote it out.

"You get uglier by the mile," Molly said. "You get bitch-slapped by a knife rack?"

He took the package of tie wraps from the backpack and tossed it across. "Lay down and zip your ankles to each other, then wrist to wrist. Use two ties to secure your ankles to the desk leg."

When the sisters were bound together and to the desk, Rick Ables, Jr. backed to the sink and poured himself a glass of tap water. After a sip, he spoke to both.

"When Dad was around, all we heard about was Nam. Nam *this* and 'When I was in Nam' *that*... I've been told reen-actments will silence his beery voice for good."

"Your ghost again, right? Whispering to you in your lonely bed?"

"His big moment was aboard a B52, pulling the levers one after another on command."

"Bombs from the sky. What a brave soldier," Molly said.

Rick Ables, Jr. clenched his teeth at that and traced his sutured cheek and jaw with a finger.

"So, here's the game." He turned the 9mm on Molly.

"You're Ho," he told her.

The gun barrel swept to the left and aimed at April.

"And you'll be Chi Minh."

"You two ready for a replay of the bombing of the trail?" he asked.

He walked to the desk and picked up the five-hundred-thousand-dollar check before grinding his boot heel on

Molly's cast, cracking the fiberglass and getting a pleasant yelp of hot anguish from her.

Returning to the short hall with the backpack, he carried the ladder into the left side bedroom.

The sisters tested their binding, finding no slack to play for escape. From down the hall came the aluminum creaking of the ladder opening, followed by the clacking of the staple gun firing four times. They heard him next in the kitchen, grunting and extending the ladder legs, unable to see him from where they lay before the couch. More staples were fired, followed by his cursing under his breath as he struggled with who knew what.

When he rounded the couch, Molly and April watched in silence as he opened the ladder in the center of the room and climbed and stapled a dirt-greet parcel that resembled a hard pillow with electronics and a timer dangling.

"Whatever this is, Clance is going to come after you," April said.

"Yes. Clance, your fuck buddy. He's already enjoyed his own twitching fire dance."

"What are you talking about?" April struggled to rise, tugging viciously at her bound wrist. Molly was doing the same, but silently, her beautiful eyes narrowed to knife slits of anger aimed at Rick Ables, Jr.

He took the two bouquets from the kitchen island and dropped one on each of the sisters.

"My ghost played a movie for me with you each in a black casket and the white flowers on top. There was no practical way to bring coffins along, but this will do. I'm already smelling sweet justice. Barbeque flavored."

He shouldered the backpack and stood before the ocean view, admiring, the girls at his back.

"Wish you had a normal front door," he spoke to both

Molly and April. "I had a really cool entrance planned. Gotta run. Enjoy your eternity in Hell."

He walked back through the house and exited by the back door.

Four minutes later, the timer in the bedroom dinged, and the first gel bomb fell, landing on the foot of the bed, splashing hot flaming goo that lit the bed, floor, and furniture. Moments later, flames were licking up the walls and forming a spiral of fire across the ceiling.

Exactly one minute after the first, the second bomb fell in the kitchen, splattering appliances and the island with sticky gobs of fire.

The third aerial bombardment, a flaming gel-splattering bomb, landed in the middle of the living room, ten feet from where Molly and April were first yelling and struggling, followed by their screaming.

PART THREE

Revenge is the law of the outlaws.

~ Laura Blumenfeld

CHAPTER EIGHTEEN

The Ghost Packs Its Bags

After the check cleared, Rick packed up his few belongings and took a suite at the Daytona Beach Hilton. At Macy's in the Volusia Mall, he bought five colorful shirts, and at a kiosk along the grand stroll on the first floor, a pair of stylish Oakley sunglasses. Next stop was Jon Hall Chevrolet where the pleasant sales staff happily agreed to return his rental. He drove off the lot in a candy red Corvette Convertible 1LT.

The first hour in the Corvette was amazing, like a spiritual lift. Cruising up and down the Daytona Beach strip, he blurped the throaty exhaust at traffic lights, taking in the jealous and admiring looks from the sides of his new shades. The second hour found him running up coastal A1A, ocean at the side between Daytona and Flagler Beach.

Some of the cool buzz faded as he stopped for a late lunch at the Oceanside deck restaurant. The amount he had spent on the car and the tagged-on pricey insurance were nagging at him. Shaking it off, he walked slowly and languidly through the tourists with their sea view, taking a small rooftop table off to the side. After a few kind glances from the tables to his right, he was ignored and left to his meal—meatloaf under brown gravy and a bowl of limp buttered broccoli.

Valet parking the Vette at the Hilton, he carried his bag of new shirts to his spacious and modern and very quiet two-room suite with its ocean view from the big bed. He tried out the two televisions, considered the swimming pool and passed. Opening the room service menu, he selected his dinner and dessert for later that night. Sitting on the balcony, he watched the waves far below. Bored with that, he took a shower and put on one of the tropical shirts.

Down in McCoy's Rum Room, the hotel's elegant bar, he sat at the far end of the bar and ordered ice water, watching the local news on the only wall-mounted television not showing sports events. To his right were businessmen and vacationing couples. A gaggle of three babbling young women in fashionable apparel and jewels was enjoying a couch table at his back.

Local channel WESH-NBC News was running through the big stories of the day, pitched by two concerned and attractive faces tag-teaming the latest events. He watched through to the end—a sports round-up and the weather. There had been no mention of a house fire up north in Ormond Beach.

When the young and lovely bartender eased along and over in front of him, Rick ordered a celebratory drink. Embarrassed by his dad's drinking, he had only let alcohol touch his lips a few times at barbecues and retirement parties with his US Marshal pals.

A minute later, the bartender set a large round glass on a napkin before him. After flashing him a dazzling smile, she abandoned him for her other customers further down the bar.

Blanching at the underlay of alcohol under the fruit and chipped ice, he nonetheless finished the drink, sucking through its straw.

Over the next two hours of pretending to enjoy a baseball game on the monitor, he ordered three more. Leaning over for the bowl of crunchy party mix, he slipped off his bar stool but didn't hit the tiles. By then, his thoughts were floating nicely like a child's balloon. He began to enjoy looking at himself in the mirror; his expensive and casual floral shirt and sunglasses, never mind the gash and sutures running like a railroad track down along the left side of his face. It made him look mysterious. Feeling cocky, he waved the bartender over.

The beautiful young thing was both slutty and somehow elegant.

"Thinking of buying a boat anchored on the Halifax River," he told her, hearing his thick tongue and ignoring it.

"Great." She flashed a smile before turning around to fill a beer stein from the tap.

Rising from his seat, he eyed her rear, not seeing that she was watching him in the mirror.

"Become a cool member of the Halifax Yacht Club," he went on, anyway.

"Lucky you." She started down the bar with the stein.

"Do you like to party?" His words trailed her. She didn't reply.

***

He woke up cold and with a sore back, laying on the lounge chair of his sea-view balcony, wearing the complimentary bathrobe. His head was thick and dull from drink, and for once, he had no memory of dreams or conversations or instructions from his holy ghost.

"Second night. Where are you?" he asked his lifelong companion.

He received nothing but silence.

The rising sun climbing out of the Atlantic splashed hard light in his face.

"Did the drinking scare you away?" he asked.

Getting no answer, he remembered his father's talk of post-battle funk, described as the old man talked into his beer can.

"Fucking loser." He shut it off and forced his body up and wandered back inside.

"Maybe a road trip?" he asked, standing in the warm water shower.

While he waited, he shampooed and rinsed his tender head.

"Whatcha think?" he pressed, starting to lose his patience. Washing his body, he listened for the ghost to gift him with a response.

"Enjoy the wind in my hot red Corvette," he went on. "Meet a new hottie every night. Talk up some waitresses and sweep them away."

Back in the bedroom, he pulled on a new silk shirt with a pattern of oranges and bananas.

"What do you think about seeing the west coast of Florida? Or heading down to those island bridges to the Keys?"

It felt like he was talking to himself. Pissed off, he ordered a man-size breakfast from room service. An hour later, he pulled four-hundred dollars from the hotel ATM and got the Vette brought around front.

"Gonna talk to me or no?" he groused at the sky, steering down the ramp for North Atlantic Avenue. Braking and holding his foot on the peddle, he waited, listening.

"Take your fucking time," he growled a minute later. "I've only got the rest of my life to plan."

CHAPTER 19

Allison

From the top of the basement stairs, Allison stared through the half-open door for the moment the man with the pistol was close enough to attack with the pipe wrench he held. The problem was the distance from the hall to where the man was climbing down the ladder in the living room. When the guy shouldered his backpack and started through the kitchen to leave, Allison decided not to take him on, but instead wait until he left to go to the voices of the sisters, who he couldn't see.

The back door closed, and he stepped out fast. There was an explosion from one of the bedrooms across from him, knocking him off his feet. All he could see was flames. A second explosion went off from somewhere up the hall, followed by a third a moment later.

Seeing the fire and smoke filling April's front room, he bashed open the door to the bathroom and cranked the taps.

"I'm coming. Stay low!" he yelled, running up the hall with soaked towels.

———

An hour later, Allison unlocked the steel door to the hurricane room and put his shoulder to it. It opened to a view of smoking, burning timbers, and piles of smoldering black destruction. The sisters followed him from the steel box, holding onto each other. Both were still draped in the soaked beach towels he had thrown over them after cutting the zip ties and guiding them through the burning house.

Standing in the smoking rubble of the garage, he asked, "And now?"

They had had plenty of time to discuss the 'who.'

"Klave's, for starters," Molly said.

The three walked shoulder to shoulder from the ruins of April's house and up the sand path to Molly's place.

"I didn't see that coming," April said halfway along. "Not from him. I'm thinking he had a brain snap."

They entered the warehouse and shop by the rear door and passed through Allison and Molly's work area, finding David Klave in his office, phone on speaker with a pen in hand. Looking up and seeing the sisters wearing ash-smudged damp towels, he ended the call.

"Was talking to fire and rescue. They're on their way. One of my guys spotted the fire. You okay?"

"We're fine, but sure as hell they'll bring the police along," Molly said.

"Yes. Them. What do you need?"

"Can I borrow a laptop?" April asked.

"And a boat?" Molly said.

David Klave unplugged his old and smudged laptop and handed it across with the power cord.

"And the Ethernet and USB cables, please," April asked.

Allison left the office and returned a minute later with a handful of paint stir sticks and a roll of duct tape to repair

Molly's broken cast. David Klave had swung around in his office chair to study the whiteboard with the lists of boats under repair and in storage.

"Long range, right?" he asked over his shoulder. "Enough boat for a few nights?"

"Yes..." April said, "... and someone to, what, drive it?"

"Captain, yes." Klave stood and shouted out into the shop, "Navarro!"

Nineteen-year-old Roberto Navarro appeared in the door a minute later, a short and well-muscled young man with a slow sweeping gaze.

"Yes, David?" he asked.

"You okay with a few days at sea? Girlfriend be all right with that?"

"Yes, of course. When?"

"Within the hour." Klave looked at the whiteboard again. "Let's drop John Clarke's boat in. He's two months in arrears. Full tanks and food and all for what, four people?" He looked to Molly.

"Three. Allison is staying back."

Allison had taken a chair opposite Klave's desk and with a borrowed pencil and pad was making a list. He nodded to the news, not looking up.

"Call your girl," Klave told Navarro. "Let's get Molly and April out of here before the badges arrive."

Molly took the chair beside Allison and looked the list over. Seeing 'new IDs' and the bulleted list of statements planned to deny being present at the fire, she added, "Please get us new bank cards and continue prepping the bike for the Santa Cruz."

"I don't know the laws..." Klave spoke to Navarro, "... but getting out of the US waters has to be a good idea. Make sure the Clarke boat has deep-sea charts."

"Got it." Navarro left to get the boat rolled out from storage and fueled and supplied.

"David, can you loan us some cash?" April asked.

"Yes, sure. How much?"

"A thousand?"

"Ouch. Yes." He swiveled and bent over to the office safe.

Cash in hand, April left the office with David Klave and walked through the shop past the crew at work. They stepped out into the heat of the day. Molly stayed behind at Allison's side. Taking his hand, she raised it to her neck.

"You were simply brilliant. No words can express, but... you have my heart. And thank you."

"See you in Santa Cruz if not sooner," Allison spoke to the warmth of her throat on his skin.

"Yes. And someday, whatever you want."

"I'll hold you to that." He smiled, his eyes rising to hers.

When Molly joined April and Klave, the thirty-one-foot amateur fishing boat was in the water, Navarro behind the wheel of the trailer truck, and three employees unloading food cases from a dolly and passing them along. A fourth man was at the pump fueling the tanks.

The burning sun was just over the treetops on the opposite shore of the Halifax River, painting the boat a warm, calming orange tint.

"She's rough-looking, but Dennis has everything maintained and serviced," Klave told the sisters, looking at the once pristine white boat showing signs of neglect—waterline stains and rust trails from the metal workings and cleats.

Navarro drove the truck and trailer up the ramp and parked on the side lot, returning as the last case of supplies was handed down. He carried a charting binder found in the office bookshelf.

"Thanks, brother." David Klave shook his hand.

April walked the length of the boat and turning around, looked at the transom.

"*She Got The House*," she read.

"And she's going to get the boat if Clarke doesn't settle up." Klave grinned, pulling on his shades for the bright low sun.

Navarro helped the sisters aboard and took in and coiled the cleat line from Dennis, who tossed him the stern rope first. From the east, the wailing, sweeping sirens of fire engines carried.

"Better late than..." David Klave used the arch of his boot to shove the boat off.

"Get them twelve miles out," he told Navarro. "No calls until then."

"On it." Navarro took in the bowline before climbing to the flying bridge and starting the twin inboard engines. As the boat backed out into the channel of slow blue waters, Molly formed a gun with her good hand, aimed it at David Klave, and fired, "Thank you, David. I'll settle up as soon as we can."

"I know you will. Get a good way away. I'm going to gather the guys and get our story straight."

"You're the best."

"I know it. Now run."

CHAPTER 20

She Got The House

Navarro cruised the white fishing boat south on the Halifax River as it merged into the Atlantic Intracoastal Waterway. Their fortune was the approaching nightfall and running with the tide. There were few boats out as he navigated into the Ponce Inlet that led to the open sea. Out in the inlet, the stone seawall ran to their left and blinking buoys to the right. He aimed straight and true for the deep eastern waters.

Setting the throttle to a smooth nine knots, he did the math, and deducting for the north running Gulf Stream, set a course. He was confident that he'd have the Danser women in international waters before darkness fell. With the electronic compass running, he maintained radio and GPS silence.

"We'll be a safe distance in less than two hours," he called down to April, who was sitting on the stern fiberglass bench, holding the closed laptop to her chest and looking at their trailing wake. With the coming nightfall, the winds were slackening, and there were few whitecaps.

"Thank you," she called back. "You're a gift."

"If it's okay with you, I'll sleep days, and you and Miss Molly can have the night."

"That's fine." She smiled up to the nineteen-year-old.

Over the next hour and a half, no one spoke. Darkness brought a scatter of brilliant stars.

Standing up, April entered the salon where she overheard her sister and Navarro chatting on the radio.

Molly was down below at the galley table absently chewing saltines from a box. "If you didn't hear, we're in safe waters."

"I heard. Guess it's beddy-bye time."

The forward berth was shaped like a pie slice, forming to the lines of the bow. The sisters climbed in together and lay shoulder to shoulder under the blankets.

"I know we burned Rick, Jr., but..." April whispered into her pillow, "... I didn't see him capable of such madness. Of coming at us like that. Gonna kick off your boots?"

"Nope."

"I'm thinking he has a dose of 'unhinged revenge.'"

"I'm going with 'one twisted bad fuck with brain worms.'"

April reached up and killed the dome light. The boat smoothed gracefully up a swell.

"Think it's true about Clance?" April asked into the darkness.

"I think it's possible. Probable. I'm so sorry."

"I've been calling him for days. Leaving messages."

Molly replied by turning around and embracing April from behind. She felt her sister's body tremble and pulled her closer.

"That sack of worms was probably lying. Big bad talk. Bluster, nothing more."

"Could be. I'll try and go with that."

———

The sisters woke at first light. April made coffee in the tin percolator atop the two-burner stove while Molly lay awake, her black boots sticking out from the covers.

"Hungry?" April called to her.

"Not even..." Milly swung her legs out of bed, "... but that smells heavenly."

After they both drank a quick cup, April joined Navarro at the helm.

"Thank you," she told him. "Now it's your beddy-bye time."

"First, let me show you our heading and the throttles," he said, leaning to the side of the wheel. "We're only trying to hold position against the stream."

Molly was stirring around down below. April and Navarro heard her moving things about and cursing.

"What's she up to?" Navarro asked.

"Fist fight with her demons. Now teach me how the electronics work."

Down below, Molly searched the galley's refrigerator and click lock cabinets before starting in on the cases of food and supplies put aboard the boat by Klave. Finding no alcohol, she considered taking a shower, looking in on the coffin-size fiberglass shell.

Turning away, she went out on the deck and stood at the side of the helm.

"Stop the boat," she asked.

April slid the throttle levers into neutral, and the boat slowed to a stop on the gentle, blue swells.

"What's up?" April asked her.

"Are you okay?" Navarro tried to catch Molly's eyes.

Ignoring them both, she climbed up onto the gunwale and dove into the sea.

Surfacing with a shake of her *Moe* wig, she swam leisurely back to the boat.

Navarro set the rail ladder in place for her and watched her climb out, her sensual body painted by her dripping wet silk dress of blue with sun dots. She sat on the bench and unlaced her boots while Navarro went down below, returning with a towel.

"A gentleman as well? Thank you." She looked him eye to eye, also taking in his nearly handsome, tan face.

"You're welcome. A hot cocoa?"

"Yum. With extra sugar, please."

In the galley, he put on a kettle of water and opened two cans of Dinty Moore beef stew and put them to simmer in a pot. He served Molly her cocoa and April a bowl of stew before returning to eat his breakfast below, out of their presence.

"Navarro? Come sit with us," Molly called. "We don't bite... hard."

The three breakfasted on the stern deck before Navarro collected the cup and bowls to wash them before going to bed.

"You're a darling, you know that?" Molly told him.

"I do, actually, but thank you for reminding me."

April laughed, pleased with Navarro's surprising rejoinder. She followed him inside and returned with her borrowed laptop and collection of cables. While she explored the array of electronics on the top and side of the helm, Molly went inside the galley.

"Ta-da," she called before coming out, having found two Halloween bags of little Skittle packs. She opened the first, took the bench across from April, and poured the small round candies into her hand.

"Good night, ladies," Navarro called over his shoulder, heading off for some well-deserved sleep.

"Nighty, night," April called back, keeping an eye on the

compass and searching the radio and other devices for a USB or Ethernet port to connect to.

"Well, this is a bust." She gave up.

"Which one of us do you think Navarro will fall for?" Molly chewed candy while tipping her boots over.

"I bet on me. You make him smile but frighten him."

"I agree."

"I'm worried sick about Clance. And our finances."

"I know." Molly peeled off her wet dress and lay it out on the deck to dry.

She joined her sister on the helm bench, naked but sun-dried. She distracted April by asking to be shown how to keep the boat going. April did so, and the two remained at the lower helm for a half hour before April went inside with the laptop and cables to explore the electronics bay above the left bench.

While Navarro slept the day away, Molly ate Skittles and played skipper. April figured out how to cable the laptop to the boat's KVH Mini-VSAT. After ten minutes of trial and error, she got a slow but reliable internet connection via the SAT orb mounted atop the flying bridge.

Her first task was using the dark web 'Kill-It' application, kicking off a hard drive triple scrub of the computers left behind in the wreckage of her home. While it would only work if the machines weren't dead *and* still able to connect, it was worth a try. With that running, she linked to her TOR version of Carbonite cloud archives, searching back to the year and time frame of the Rick hit. She launched a data dump which began running painfully slow.

Out at the helm, she butt-bumped Molly and sat down beside her.

"Lunch?"

Molly held up her bag of Halloween candy.

"I'm going with stew. Saw we have a case of the stuff," April said.

"Your ideas on Jr.? I'm thinking squashed like a cockroach."

"Yes, of course. You think on that. I'm going after his old banking records, but that's only a start."

"Will do. It's a fine distraction. I wouldn't mind a couple of fifths of Tanqueray."

"You hold yourself together. Your stronger than that stuff."

"Yes, I think I am."

April got up and washed herself and her white shorts and t-shirt in the aft deck open-air shower and pulled them back on. Molly pulled on her dried dress while April headed inside for the case of Dinty Moore.

———

Navarro appeared early evening, and the three had dinner together at the galley table, two more cans of beef stew and bottled water, Molly staying with Skittles. She headed off to bed not long after.

At ten o'clock that night, the moon rose out of the ocean, full and innocently white, coming up out of the black sea and rising into the black sky. April climbed around to the bow of the boat and sat in full view.

"I'm thinking I'm afraid to go to shore," she told the moon.

Looking up along the silver path lying on the water, she listened to the engines purring and vibrating the fiberglass under her rear.

"Safe in the middle of nowhere. This could work."

Days and months and years on the endless glistening silver road, the moon was lying out across the swells.

"Bozo idea but attractive." She felt the forward view starting to hypnotize her.

"E-nough." She shook her head and rose to go sink into the land of dreams under warm blankets.

Somewhere in the middle of the night, she was woken by the sounds of Molly opening cabinets and rustling through the supply boxes. Her thoughts were tangled with sadness and conflicting images. Ignoring Molly's cursing as she searched in vain for booze, she spoke to the ceiling low over her head.

"Clance, I'm so sorry."

———

An hour after sunrise the next morning, April was at her laptop on the galley table, Molly stirring in their pie-slice bed. Having only one computer, April was scratching quick notes on a legal pad found in a drawer. She didn't look up from her work when her sister slid in beside her.

Molly took a sip of April's coffee, saying, "more sugar."

"Got Jr.'s banking info, including the card details from when you flipped it."

"Well done. Can you get our money back?"

"Not yet, it's unfrozen but there's a hold. This snail-pace connection isn't helping. I did see that there's 66K in our account he didn't get to."

"I've been thinking, closing in on a plan," Molly said.

"Tell me."

Before Molly could go on, Navarro opened the salon door.

"Good morning, Miss April and Miss Molly. I hope you slept well?" Navarro stepped down into the galley. He opened two cans of stew and put the pot on the back burner. Molly left April at the table and joined Navarro.

When the stew was bubbling, Molly leaned into Navarro's arm.

"I'll try a bowl, too, please," she said.

"Of course, be just another minute."

"We okay with fuel?" Molly asked.

"We're okay for two more days. Then, yes, we'll need fuel. And stores."

"Can we take care of that today?"

April set her pencil down and looked over, head tilted but not questioning.

"Yes, of course." Navarro leaned away to get three bowls from the cabinet over the sink. Molly got spoons from the drawer at his hip.

After breakfast, Molly washed the dishes before following April and Navarro topside. April took the helm, and Molly stepped out into the morning breeze, raising her face to the warm morning sun. The boat was motoring smooth and sure in the swells like rolling blue knolls.

"Going to shower and sleep," Navarro told the sisters.

Molly joined April at the helm seat as he started the aft deck shower and hung his shirt on a hook.

April turned to watch Navarro soaping up in the shower, keeping his trunks on, the rolling blue sea in the background.

"Sis, put your eyes back in," Molly teased.

"Teach me the all of the boat?" April elbowed Molly while calling over to Navarro, "I might buy one. I'm liking this twelve-mile life."

"If you like, yes, of course." Navarro rinsed shampoo from his face.

The sisters watched him turn off the taps and dry his hair, face, and chest with his shirt.

"Can you message Allison?" Molly asked. "Tell him I need two 9mms, extra clips, and a couple of boxes of rounds."

"What are you cooking up?" April asked.

"Not saying yet. It's still coming together."

"Yes, already asked him to go to work on new bank cards and checkbooks."

"And you? What's in your brain?"

"Also thinking it through. I'm liking this boating life."

"Can you make money out here?"

"Slowly, but yes, it looks so. Scoot." April nudged Molly, who stood and let her slide out.

When Navarro stepped from the shower, April took his arm for the first time. Eyeing the row of pole holders on the transom rail, she asked him, "Can we catch a fish? And eat it?"

"If we buy bait, poles, and weights, yes."

"I'm liking it. Molly, did you hear that?"

"Yes, gorgeous. Another reason to go to shore. Today."

"This evening, please. I need to sleep," Navarro said.

"Of course. You sleep, and we'll run the boat."

Navarro headed below, and April went to stand behind Molly, resting her chin on her shoulder.

"Not going to shore for a drink, right?" she asked her sister.

"Not even." Molly leaned away and turned around. Her lovely eyes tightened down before she spoke.

"Going hunting."

CHAPTER 21

Nowhere and More Nowhere

Rick Ables, Jr. kept the Corvette at ninety miles per hour across the middle of endless and bland Florida. He was still getting a slight buzz when he got looks from another car as he powered past in his cool shirt and hot red ride. It was a burning hot day with winds. Wisps of sand smoke were brushing across Interstate 4, swirling low across the paving.

"Whoa," he said, seeing that the gas hungry Vette was near 'E' again. He began studying the endless rows of hundred-foot pines, the only variance being sections of highway where ivy had taken ahold of the trees climbing from one to another.

Seven miles later, he saw a road sign for food and fuel.

"There we go."

He ran the Vette up to a hundred miles per hour before having to back off for the exit. Yet another highway gasoline and fast food island. Pulling on his sharp Oakley sunglasses, he strolled across to the gas station's mini-mart rather than pay at the pump, hoping for envious looks at his hot car and cool and casual saunter. The bored and half-asleep cashier took his cash without so much as a "hello" or "thanks."

Back on the road, he continued his aimless crisscrossing of northern Florida.

"Nowhere and more nowhere." He turned on the stereo, hoping some music would lift his spirits.

The *Jack and the Bear* radio show came on, playing old and scratchy vaudeville songs of bright melodies and dark, sexually suggestive lyrics. He hummed along not knowing the words.

When the show ended in a cascade of commercials, he turned the stereo off. An hour into the following silence, he turned his eyes skyward. Suspecting the answer, he nonetheless asked,

"Going to talk to me?"

Ten minutes later, having heard nothing more than the wind swirling the interior of the convertible, he decided to follow the sun low in the sky, figuring it would somehow get him to the gulf coast.

The endless miles of pines along both sides of the highway were interrupted at times by billboards when towns approached. Seeing signs with beach towns listed, he slowed up and cruised at eighty-five.

The nicest hotel he could find was the Holiday Inn Express on I-75 in Tampa. He took the three-room, presidential suite, two hundred and sixty dollars and change per night. The lobby was empty, the desk clerk readily smiling but not reacting to his cool appearance. She did take in the sutured side of his face but didn't comment.

The suite was modern and clean and strikingly quiet. Taking a cozy chair, he opened the hotel's binder of services, flipping through the many amenities. The place had a pool and all the usual trappings as well as nearby restaurants and all. None of it interested him except the complimentary high-speed Wi-Fi. Turning on the television, he left the news running in the front room and ran the shower and undressed.

"Squashed them." He raised his face into the stream, hoping to lift his doldrums. He grinned rather than smiled into the water.

"Got a shitload of money."

It was a nice reminder but didn't provide the rush it had before. In the front room, he sat naked at the desk, drawing up a shopping list on hotel stationery.

---CVS for more Neosporin and scar cream for another batch of goo.

---Macy's if there is one in Tampa for some sporty and cool long shorts.

---Dinner.

That was it. There was the rest of his evening and night.

Shaking his head to chase off the frustrating thoughts of another night alone, he retrieved his laptop from his backpack and connected to Wi-Fi and kicked off a new search for Volusia county.

Endless announcements of weekend festivals and arts and crap sidewalk fairs were followed by sports and weather. He navigated to the Crime page, ignoring the past week's display of mugshots of the arrested. Scrolling down, he clicked on *Mysterious House Fire Near Ormond Beach.*

Daytona Beach News-Journal

Deputies: Mysterious House fire near Ormond Beach By Lizbeth Randal

Posted August 28, 2018 at 3:50 PM, Updated August 28, 2018 at 8:44 PM

Fire Investigators are perplexed by the cause of the fire that destroyed a residence on Windswept Road north of Ormond Beach, the Volusia County Sheriff's Office said.

Tuesday's fire occurred around six in the evening, leaving the house burned to its foundation. Apparently, a well-orchestrated attack on the unoccupied home, three napalm-like fires were ignited. Investigators found two melted timing devices used to start the fires and have sent samples of the flammable gel to the state laboratories. A property title search shows the missing owners as April Danser, 29, and Molly Danser, 29, whereabouts unknown.

"We're hoping to confirm the owners' safety and interview them," the Volusia County Sheriff's Office said. Records show that the two women also own Klave's Boat Repair and Storage on the adjoining property, which was untouched by the fire.

"Our preliminary belief is that this is an act of arson, reason unknown," said sheriff's spokeswoman, Lana Willows.

Anyone with information is urged to call the Sheriff's Office at 386-248-1777 or Crime Stoppers of Northeast Florida at 1-888-277-TIPS.

The brief article was under a photograph of the fire-ravaged cinder block foundations.

"How?" was his first reaction to the news of the sisters' survival, seeing them still zip- tied on the floor and secured to the heavy desk. He lifted the laptop wanting to throw it, his breathing taxed, his face hot and flushed.

Lowering the computer, he read through the article two more times, looking for any bit that he could get his hooks into and follow up on.

"Fucking nothing."

He launched another search looking for other news on the fire.

There was none.

Closing the laptop, he stood, turning a half circle, his eyes narrowed and teeth clenched. Seeing his shopping list on the desk, he took up the pen and added a line.

---*The other half of the property. That boat place. Jam them up. See what song they sing.*

Tilting his head back in the middle of the room, he found a smile and let it painfully stretch his injured cheek and jaw.

"The hunt is back on." He thanked the popcorn texture of the hotel suite ceiling.

Dressing quickly, he packed up and pocketed his wallet and car keys. Walking across the lobby, he recalled one of the jaunty melodies from the *Jack and the Bear* radio show. Still humming the tune, five minutes later, he steered the Corvette out into the evening.

CHAPTER 22

Happy Hunting

With Navarro standing at her back, April navigated the boat south and west across wind-licked and royal blue swells. They were up on the flying bridge, which offered the best view of all four sides of the *She Got The House*. He had turned on the navigation electronics and the GPS display offering a top-down display of their course back to Ponce Inlet.

They made the Halifax Harbor Marina three hours later.

Navarro coached April, and she slow and carefully navigated the harbor waters, learning the meaning of the buoys and right-of-way among the other boats. She brought them in without incident or alarm to the fuel dock, where they tied the boat off, and Navarro walked her through the steps to refuel. A quarter-hour later, they were tied off in a visitor slip.

"I've drawn up a shopping list," Navarro said. "Come along?"

"Thank you. I will next time. Molly and I need to talk." April peeled off two hundred dollars and handed him the rest.

Pocketing the cash, Navarro walked off and up the dock

to buy supplies, April calling after him, "A change of clothes, please."

His hand went up, thumb extended.

Molly came up topside, looking rested and calm.

"You sure you don't want to come home with me?"

"I'm sure. I am liking this boat life more and more. Let's get out of the sun. I need to show you what we have on Jr."

April pushed her laptop aside on the galley table and spread out a worn map of Florida found in the boat's charting binder. Molly sipped bottled water as April explained.

"As of this morning, he's down to 421K."

Molly did the math.

"What did he do with the rest?"

"Jon Hall Chevrolet. Ass clown bought a toy. Won't get to enjoy it for long."

"I'm working on getting his balance to zero," April looked pleased and focused, leaning to the map pit before them.

"From his recent card use..." April tapped the map with her fingertip and drew a line and then a circle in between it. "The asswipe ran across the state east to west and is now spinning around in the middle. His last purchase was near Tampa."

"Nicely done, sis."

"I sent Allison a message to get you a burner. I'll keep tracking Jr. and message you."

"I want to stop him. Hard."

"And we will."

April handed over their last two hundred dollars. "Cash for your Uber plus a bit."

Molly took April's arm and laid her head on her shoulder.

"You're a wonder. Hope you know that," she said.

"I do."

They shared a smile before Molly slid out off the bench. April followed her up and out on the aft deck.

"We *could* just let him go," April said. "He's not worth your getting hurt or arrested."

"Yes, we could, but... you start making us some big money again. I'll be fine."

The sisters embraced. April stood at the back of the boat watching Molly walk up the dock until she disappeared beyond the rows of masts for the parking lot.

———

The Uber driver pulled off John Anderson Drive and into Klave's parking lot, back of the boat ramp. She got out, paid the driver, and wove through the boats under repair out front.

"Hey, hey," she called to the guys at the shaded table enjoying an afternoon break. Heads turned, smiles were offered, and soda cans were raised. David Klave stood and crossed.

"How's our favorite lovely?" he greeted her.

"Sober and cranky." She tiptoed and kissed his cheek.

"Fire and police have been by twice. We've been a bunch of know-nothings."

"Thank you."

"Where's the boat?"

"April still has it. She's back up and running, and we'll be flush again soon."

"Good. Bills are stacking up. You know we'll have to start a Navarro and April rumor."

They exchanged a smile, eye to eye.

"How can you not? Just don't let it get to his sweetheart."

"Promise."

"Got to go work with Allison. Thank you again." She headed inside the shade of the three-story building.

Allison was at his second workbench rebuilding the brakes for her race bike.

"Good to see you," he welcomed her, setting his tools aside. "Doing okay?"

"Doing fine."

"Your docs and all are on the other table."

She took his arm, and they walked over together to take a look.

The 9mm lay beside two extra clips and a box of ammo. She saw the new checkbook and debit card and picked up the newly minted driver's license.

"Lydia Deetz."

"The goth girl in *Beetlejuice*. You remind me of her. You're sexier, though."

"Thank you for that." She noted the hair and eye color.

"Back in a bit," she went on. "Need a shower and, oh Lordy, fresh clothes."

She climbed upstairs to her loft for a shower and change of clothing and to pack a bag. To match her new ID, she put in sea blue eyes and pulled on one of her brunette wigs—the brushed back, shoulder-length one.

Back downstairs with no bikes available except the modified Vespa, she pointed to the middle of her three cars. Allison helped her pull the dust cover off her midnight silver station wagon, a 2014 Mercedes-Benz.

"I fueled all three, not knowing." Allison opened the car door for her.

"My Allison, always five steps ahead."

While he rolled up the rear door, she collected the gun and all into her bag and climbed into the car. Backing out into the hot day, she dropped the passenger window.

"See you soon," she called to him. "Got a bug to squash."

"Be safe and happy hunting."

CHAPTER 23

Broke

Rick Ables, Jr. drove west to east on Highway 4, the headlights piercing the night and keeping him aimed at his new goal—waiving his handgun and expired ID at Klave's until he knew where the two cunts were.

"*Gibsonia*? The fuck?" he read the next town's name on a passing road sign and while not interested in visiting that town, he lifted off the gas for the ramp, seeing a towering gasoline sign.

Under the painful bright sodium lights, he slid his debit card into the pump, about to take the gas cap off when he saw the odd message displayed.

Please See Cashier.

He slid his card in and out a second time. Got the same message. Grabbing his cell phone off the passenger seat, he looked out past the glaring white lighting from above into the palmetto and oak trees bordering the gas station.

"This smells bad," he spoke to the view before opening his phone.

Logging into his banking application, he clicked and scrolled until the message was clear.

Insufficient Funds.

He cocked his arm, ready to throw the phone and caught himself just in time. Tapping the call icon, let it ring twice until it rolled to voicemail. He pulled out his wallet and counted through the cash.

"Not enough for another hotel." He took out two twenties and walked for the glass doors of the station's mini-mart.

After topping off the gas-guzzling Vette, he had enough cash for a couple of drive-thru fast meals and another tank of fuel.

Back out on the highway, he kept his pace at the speed limit for the first time, trying to conserve. Twisting his hands into the wheel, his eyes narrowed as he stared straight into the distance.

"Drop Molly first." He looked up into the sky, forcing a smile, listening for encouragement.

Hearing nothing but wind, he gave in to the impulse to accelerate the car.

"Then the other, after she's written another check. Soon as that clears, she gets a private fire."

Reaching Ormond Beach at two in the morning, he pulled off into a lot for beach parking, buttoned his seat back, and tried to find sleep as uncomfortable as he was.

"Going to be a busy day," were his last words before he closed his eyes.

CHAPTER 24

"You injured? We fight for you."

Day turned into evening as Molly drove west, the low orange sun close to blinding. Pulling off into a food and fuel turnout as the sun set, she climbed out into the muggy heat. While refueling the Mercedes wagon, she messaged April.

Molly: *In Tampa. Next stop, that Holiday Inn. Any line on what he's driving?*

April's response came in as Molly was placing the nozzle back to the pump.

April: *Nothing. Dipsticks sold him the car won't say.*

Molly climbed into the car and typed.

Molly: *Some good news. Got you a new client. Saw 'You injured? We fight for you.'*

Molly entered the billboard attorney's name and number. April replied before she could hit send.

April: *Big toothed smile, I assume?*
Molly: *Yep, and the hairstyle. It is a wonder.*
April: *How you going to play the hotel?*

Molly: *Weepy confused wife. All I need is his room number. Knock, knock, look who's dying painfully.*

April: *Don't go in angry. Better to shoot him from behind.*

Molly: *You're right.*

Molly got back inside the car and headed for the Holiday Inn Express, following the highway signs.

"She's right, but I want to see his expression," she said to herself. With one hand on the wheel, she hefted her bag from the passenger seat liking the weight of the gun and ammo.

It was dark when she pulled into the hotel. Under the dome light, she filled two clips and jacked one of them into the 9mm. Studying the lights of the lobby entrance, she took two calming breaths she didn't need. Her path and intention were cold-blooded and clear—one to the chest and two to the head after he was down. Stroll casually out a side exit, jump back on the highway, and head south to dust the trail, assuming anyone saw her.

She was getting out of the car when her phone dinged.

April: *Got into his phone. Turn around. His last call places him here."*

CHAPTER 25

Things to Do

Hunkered over her laptop, April sent the 'turn around' message and held her breath. She had Jr.'s phone account open in one window and her and Molly's texting app running in another.

"Know anyone who can get me a gun or rifle?" she asked Navarro, who was opening yet another two cans of beef stew for a late-night dinner.

"Not even. Best I can do is the fish-cleaning knife."

"We have a flare gun?"

"Yes, in the emergency kit."

"Get it for me, please."

Navarro turned the burner off and went and got the gun from the lower helm kit box. April stared down the texting app, willing it to give her Molly's reply. She heard Navarro lay the flare gun on the table to her right, followed by the clicking of bowls and spoons being set out.

She ate a few bites of the very familiar stew while pulling over her notepad and pencil. Flipping over the page where she had scribbled the billboard lawyer's information, she wrote, interrupted only by continued glances at the texting application.

---*One: Warn Klave*
  ---*Two: Warn Allison*
  ---*Three: Lose Navarro for his own safety*

Standing from the table, she picked up the four flare gun cartridges and placed them in the breast pocket of the oversized white shirt Navarro had bought her. The gun went into her shorts pocket.

Joining Navarro at the lower helm, she studied the glowing electronics. The night had a chill, and she rolled down her shirt sleeves.

"Missing your honey?" she asked.

"A lot, yes."

"Good for you. And her. Change in plans. We're heading back to shore."

"Thank you. Are you okay with waiting for daylight?"

"That's fine. I've got things to do." April headed back to her computer and notebook on the galley table.

Adding a new item to list, she couldn't help but grin.

---*Four: Buy a couple of shovels and pick a spot.*

CHAPTER 26

School's in Session

His eyes feeling gritty and red, Rick Ables, Jr. woke up, straightened his seat, and glared back at the blinding sun inches above the shimmering Atlantic. His back hurt almost as much as the cuts and gashes. The Vette rumbled to life.

Wanting a man-size breakfast, he pulled out of the sandlot and onto A1A. A couple of miles up the road, he spotted Alfie's diner and slowed. Turning on the blinkers, he waited impatiently while a slow three-car train passed in the opposite direction.

From out of nowhere, he was washed by a chill.

"Well, hello there. Glad you're back." He looked up into the sky.

The image of his plate of pancakes, sausage, eggs, and toast evaporated. In its place, the angry tumbling clouds resembled a dog-headed beast with its fangs bared.

"Looking good," Rick said, feeling inspired, his confidence and backbone stiffening.

"Glad you decided to come along to play," he added. "It's our big day."

Turning the blinker off, he gave the Vette a hefty kick in the ass with his foot on the accelerator, burning tire marks in the pavement. Untamed low foliage streamed past on his left, the ocean to his right. Running north, he squinted forward, looking for the road to the sister's place.

Ten minutes later, he turned onto Windswept Road and let it lead him past the blackened ruins of their home all the way to John Anderson Road that ran alongside the Halifax River.

Parked alongside an untamed hedge in the shade of a hundred-year oak, he was thirty yards from the boat shop, close enough for a good view of the docks and big open door with the blue river to his left.

"Let's stir in a dab of revenge and a splash of justice," he spoke to his holy ghost. Its razor-sharp claws had a strong purchase deep into the meat of his left shoulder.

He studied the men opening the shop for the day. They looked sleepy and happy and without a clue about how their lives were about to go from bland to nightmarish.

"Your lunchbox daydream is about to end," he said, turning to his backpack on the passenger seat.

A silver station wagon rolled past and turned into the boat repair shop. He watched it park and the door open.

When Molly got out of the car, he climbed out of his, Glock in hand, sliding two spare clips into his pocket.

Approaching slowly, he got a couple of casual glances from the employees. He was holding the gun at his back. Pasting on a bemused smile, he shrugged before raising his free hand, saying, "Hello. Can you help me?"

Molly hadn't spotted him yet. She was walking to the big, handsome older man in a spotless polo shirt.

Being so close to her, his brain lit up, and his vision

narrowed like he was staring through a red-tinged tunnel. His intended cool and calm went up in flames.

Sucking in a deep breath, he tried in vain to try to extinguish the worst of it. Needing to aim accurately, he growled.

"Gonna rub her nose in it," he growled over his shoulder to his partner.

Improvising as he had been trained in the Marshal Service, he decided to wave the other guy off and drop Cunt One, wishing Cunt Two was around to watch.

First, he needed Molly to turn and recognize him.

"School's in session!" he roared.

CHAPTER 27

Collision

At the top helm, April guided the *She Got The House* up the Halifax River, Navarro standing at her back, watching on silently. She rolled back the throttles as Klave's came into view—the docks appearing first, extended out over the smooth waters.

She heard Jr.'s crazed voice, sounding over the top unhinged, screaming something about 'school.' Staring at the entrance to the boatyard, there he was with what looked like a gun held at his back, swinging it around.

"Teaching you a lesson," he yelled.

Grabbing the flare gun from her bag, she thumbed the safety off, aimed and fired. The bright tracer shot glowed hot red as it skimmed across the water and road. Missing Jr. by a foot, the fiery red bullet struck and splashed against the hull of a trailered ski boat.

Jr. ducked away, caught his balance, and looked at the burning, glowing boat and then out to the river. He brought the handgun the rest of the way around.

"Run!" April screamed across the distance.

"Setting things right!" Jr. also screamed, taking aim at Molly.

The boatyard employees were scattering and ducking, all except David Klave, bravely walking to Jr., arms out, yelling.

Jr. swung the barrel of his gun onto him.

A second later, David Klave's chest sprayed crimson as the bullet struck. The gun fired a second time, tearing off the left side of his head. He collapsed like a dropped sack of bowling balls.

Aiming to the left at Molly, Jr. pulled the trigger.

The bullet punched a hole in a pickup to her right, and she dropped and spun.

Kneeling, Molly got her gun out and opened fire. She let loose with five shots. Clambering to her feet, she ran for the big door, not looking to see if she had hit him.

Jr. followed her, aiming, letting off another round.

"You brought this on. Not my fault," he yelled, walking past David Klave's stricken body in a sure and confident stride.

Molly made the doorway and disappeared into the shadows. Jr. was on her tail, shouting, gun sweeping, finger tight on the trigger. He entered the darkness, squinting to adjust to the darkness.

A gunfight erupted. At least a dozen shots.

April made to dive from the flying bridge.

Navarro clenched her arm, shouting, "Wait!"

She glared at him, struggling to break the grip and climb the rail. He locked his hand tighter. She balled her hand into a fist and was about to swing when motion in front of the big door caught her eye.

Jr. walked out into the sunlight. Fist pumping, he looked delighted, the awful scar on the side of his face stretched in a grin.

"Use that!" Navarro looked to the flare gun in April's hand. She raised it and tracked Jr. as he walked to the boatyard exit. When he was before a shark-like black car, she pulled the trigger.

The glowing red shot crossed the distance hot and fast.

"Fuck!" she screamed.

A hedge at the front of the automobile exploded in a brilliant glow.

Jr. went down but gathered his legs and feet and got the car door open. He started the engine before looking across the road and water. As the rear tires spun and kicked up a cloud of sand, he turned away from April and steered through the sparking white smoke.

CHAPTER 28

Out to Sea

At the flying bridge, April clenched Navarro's arm, both studying the shore. Within minutes, wailing sirens were racing up the river road from both directions. The Corvette was long gone, headed north. The first of the sweeping blue and red lights were streaming in the trees, approaching fast.

"You need to get out of here. Get to the sea," Navarro told her.

"The fuck with that."

"You can't do anything in jail. Drop me off and run."

April turned the wheel to shore and nudged the throttles.

"I'll jump. Go." Not waiting for her argument, he climbed the flying bridge railing and dove.

Tears burning in her eyes, she reversed the throttle levers and backed the boat out into the channel.

"I'll do worse than drop him," she promised Molly.

Taking a final glance at Klave's, she saw one of his employees step out of the shadows, sadly shaking his head.

He caught his balance as his knees gave, his hand to the frame of the big door.

———

Back out at sea, April kept the bow pointed east until the navigation display showed that she was out beyond twelve miles from shore. Climbing down to the shade of the lower helm, she cut the engines and went inside to her laptop on the table. Staring at the screen as the computer booted, she was overcome with an outbreak of shivering.

"My Molly." Her knees began striking the underside of the table as the trembling became worse.

"You made it out, right?" she pleaded, her entire frame shaking.

Closing the laptop, she dropped to her left, brought her legs up onto the bench and curled fetal, teeth clicking, and her body quaking.

"Sure, you did, I just know it." She squeezed her eyes tight and fought the racking spasms with deep breaths that, try as she might, didn't slacken.

———

An hour later, she sat up and went to check the boat's position.

"Still in the middle of nowhere." She went back inside.

Opening her laptop, she looked around the galley, the small shoebox that was then her home.

"What to do? And why?" she whispered.

She pulled her pen and notebook over but didn't write.

———

As the sun set into the western sea, April sat at the lower helm with an unopened bottle of water. She rubbed her face with her hands, trying again to the clear the fog and lethargy that had settled over her thoughts.

"Say time will help," she asked the orange setting sun. "Say any-fucking-thing."

Half-formed plans and chores to do came to mind and dissolved in the mist.

"I'm at a loss. And so very sad."

CHAPTER 29

A Day to Do

April woke at first light, seeing she had slept on top of the bed instead of climbing in under the blankets. After putting the coffee percolator on the burner, she went and checked the boat's position at the lower helm. Starting the engines, she steered southeast in the northward Gulf Stream and watched the blue swells until the boat was pretty much in the same location as the day before.

"At least eat," she instructed herself, it being twenty-four hours or more since her last meal. Opening a can of stew, she ate it cold with a spoon while sipping coffee. Looking at the closed laptop at her elbow, she hesitated to reach for it.

"Only one way to deal with fear." She opened the lid and started the computer.

Her fingers unsteady above the keys, the vision from the previous day's nightmare came fully into view. The big dark doorway at Klave's. Her imagination ran with and gave her the rolling door crashing down and up fast like steel teeth chomping, chewing.

"Back off." Her shoulders shuddered, and she barked at the vignette.

Opening a secure internet browser, she launched the messaging application.

After addressing an email to Allison, she froze for a minute, her fingertips quivering. The three hardest words she ever typed displayed.

April: *Did she die?*

Hitting send, she stared at those three words, waiting for the reply that she couldn't *will* Allison to answer.

————

Sometime later, she opened a browser alongside the messaging application where her question to Allison still floated without an answer. The local television stations had previously recorded 'on scene' footage ripe with frightful images of Klave's with the breathless voices of newscasters. There were no details of any worth.

Opening the online *Daytona Beach News-Journal*, the story was in the banner.

Three Killed in a Possible Attempted Robbery

April read that David Klave was declared dead on the scene. She learned that Molly's pal, Dennis, was also murdered, evidence suggesting that he was trying to cover and protect another victim. No other names were offered, pending notification of next to kin. One man had been shot twice and was expected to survive. He was being attended to in the ICU at Memorial Medical Hospital. There was nothing about the third victim. No mention of Molly or her status.

She saw her own name given as one of the 'persons of interest.'

Klave's employees were quoted as saying that the suspect had a long face that was injured. He had driven off in a late model red Corvette, heading north.

She read three more news reports in the Ormond Beach, Orlando, and St. Augustine newspapers, the body count making the story a headliner. There was no additional information, only a recap and worthless commentary.

She closed the browser and looked to the messaging application.

No reply from Allison.

She sent the text again and waited ten long and painful minutes.

Leaving the table for the flying bridge, she grabbed a bottle of water and a package of the saltines she had seen her sister snacking on. The light went out over the middle of the galley as she left, and she made a mental note to put in a fresh bulb.

Up top, the breeze was sweeping away the heat of the day. She checked her location, fired the engines, and spent the next hour staring at the ocean until she had the boat back in place.

Climbing down the ladder, she went inside and saw that Allison had not replied.

"My beautiful Molly..." she held her eyes closed, "... I'm still hoping."

She spent the rest of that day at the lower helm, getting up every half hour to look for a message from Allison.

As the sun set at her back, she went inside to look again. The darkening galley reminded her to find a package of light bulbs and a step-ladder. She found both in the click-lock supply closet and had the dead bulb out and was poised to twist in the new one when it slipped from her fingers. It shattered, and she got a new one from the closet, along with the dustpan and broom. The second bulb went in easily, and she climbed down to sweep up the aluminum cone and shards.

The messaging application pinged.

Instead of hurrying to it, she stalled, fearful of the news. She finished up the sweeping and stepped to the table, the ball of her right foot landing on a stabbing missed piece of glass.

"Brilliant." She felt the deep cut as she swung around on the bench and looked to the message screen.

April: *Did she die?*

   Ali: *Don't know.*

April: *Find out.*

   Ali: *I'm on it. It is a fuck storm here. Wasn't here when it happened. Parts store.*

April: *You learn anything?*

   Ali: *Yes, of course.*

Pulling her legs up on the bench, she finger-pinched the top of the shard sticking out of the bottom of her foot. It was in an inch or more. The piece broke before sliding out, and only the top half came out. With bloody fingers, she dug and used her fingernails to try and grab the remaining glass. It was too deeply embedded.

Giving up on that, she sat staring at the computer willing it to provide news on her sister.

Around ten o'clock, she repositioned the *She Got The House* a final time for the night and hobbled to the bed in the berth, leaving blood drops and smears in her wake.

"Don't give me any more of that big chewing door," she asked the ceiling, referring to the prior night's nightmare. She slid a pillow down to Molly's side of the bed and put her arms around it, expecting and getting a fitful night of sleep.

———

The next morning greeted her with low gray fog and a listless rolling sea. She stared at the porthole window, her foot aching.

"Get up," she told herself. "Got a day to do."

She scooted to the edge of the bed, over the blood-stained bedding, and went first for the laptop.

Allison had written to her at four in the morning.

Ali: *I was interviewed by the police. Like I know anything. Learned that 3 died, but you probably know the same. Refused to give me names. They're looking for you.*

She typed.

April: *Find her.*

Locating the first-aid kit, she wound tape around a sterile pad on her foot and went and repositioned the boat.

While the sun burned off the fog by mid-morning, she put the coffee on and used the can opener on the last can of beef stew. Eating listlessly, she scrolled her computer for any new information. There were retellings with the same vague facts and nothing more.

"How do I face this?" She closed the laptop. "My darling Molly."

For something to do, she climbed up to the flying bridge. The last wisps of fog were dissolving, and the heat was climbing fast. Staring at the endless blue sea, "Can I accept this?" crossed her lips.

"Have to. I'm going to hold on."

Climbing down the ladder, she went inside and saw that Allison had not sent anything new. Back out on the deck, she stripped and washed her shirt and shorts and herself in the outdoor shower on the stern deck.

"What to do?" she said, standing naked in the sun.

She decided to stay nude and climbed to the flying bridge, finding a bit of lift in spirit with the choice. She found a tube of sunscreen in the map tube and smoothed it on her face and body.

An hour passed with her not seeing the ocean stretching forever in all four directions.

"I'm tired of you," she spoke to her own thoughts, a carousel of sadness and fear. And anger.

"Never got my fishing lesson," she spoke to the memory of the friendly and capable Navarro. "I hope you're are doing well."

She climbed down and sat at the galley table, notebook and pencil in hand.

"I'm going with her having survived," she spoke to herself. "I have to. So... back to it. Somehow."

Staring at the pencil in her hand, her thoughts unclear, still circling like a merry-go-round but mostly void of emotion and closing in on tasks.

"Nothing's coming. Yet." She stared at the blue lines of the notepad page.

Bothered by the dull throbbing from her foot, she went out on deck and tied off a bucket, dropped it over the side, and sat back on the bench with her injury soaking in the salt-water. After a half hour of that, she returned to the galley table.

There was nothing new from Allison.

An email from Jeff the Prof had come in with the subject line, *Jackpotting*. It was followed by a two-page list of links.

April spent the next hour reading about a new style of scam involving Diebold Nixdorf ATM machines hacked with a tweaked endoscope. When one was inserted into the port inside the machines, malware could be planted. Two flavors of results were available. The first was a data dump of credit card and PIN numbers. The second was sending a command that caused a jackpot of cash to spit out. She received a vision of Molly and herself in disguise, middle of the night, filling duffle bags with spilling cash.

With notes and questions penciled on the notepad, she sent Jeff a reply.

April: *I'm in. Will study this more. Do the same. Standard rate. Molly would enjoy this.*

"I'm back," she told herself. On a fresh page, she began the list of things needing to happen. It was a good place to hide from the fears about her sister.

---Return this loaner and buy myself a boat
   ---Fishing poles and gear
   ---Bait
   ---Fuel and more food (no beef stew) and more water
   ---RES more on jackpotting. Message Allison about modifying endoscopes.

A wave of sadness and fear swept over her. Gazing around the small galley, her eyes welled. She added a new line.

---Molly

She couldn't find the steps needed, only hot spinning anguish with trailing wisps of hope.

It'll come to me.

A new topic came to mind, and her pencil raced.

---Jr.

    ---An anonymous, detailed batch file to:

    ---US Marshals

    ---FBI

    ---IRS

    ---Local cops

    ---Newspaper

Her spirits lifted, she left the table and opened a can of tuna fruit cocktail and found a fork.

Out at the lower helm, she looked across to her sun-dried clothing and decided not to put them on.

"Naked pirate," she mused and got her first grin in quite a while, arching the left side of her lips.

The freedom of being childishly naked helped to dump some of the ballast of sadness. After navigating the boat back south and west to the area Navarro had trained her to maintain, she ate her lunch.

Back in safe waters, April returned to the galley table to added another line.

---Continue living.

CHAPTER 30

Oh, Molly

April was up on the top helm, a bottle of water in the cup holder, eating from a tin of bland biscuits. She had passed on the packages of crackers, having seen Molly eating from one.

"On course. Yay, me," she told the top-down navigation display. She had pulled on her shorts and shirt at nightfall, and her right foot rested in the bucket of seawater.

Clearing the Ponce Inlet at two in the morning, she turned north on the Halifax River. Under the black sky, only the running lights offering illumination forward, she steered for the docks at Klave's.

"I'd kill for binoculars." She slowed to a crawl in the channel, studying the boatyard and parking lot for possible interior lights of a police car. Idling the engines, she brought the boat to a stop in a visitor slip.

"Going with tipsy, confused yachting bimbo," she decided before climbing down to the dock in case she came upon a cop assigned to securing the crime scene. Her hands messed and stirred her wig, and she unbuttoned the shirt to her tummy.

Across the front of the shop and the yard, sagging yellow crime scene tape hung from road cones, blocking off this area and that. Climbing down onto the dock, she tied off the boat front and rear.

Her foot hurt, but she gave it no mind. Slackening her mouth and half-closing her eyes and weaving as much as walking, she went forward along the plank boards to the road and the entrance to Klave's.

The work yard was under a sodium lamp. Even after a washing, there were rust-colored bloodstains on the cement in front of the shop. The big door was closed and padlocked with a yellow tape 'X.'

"Take it *very* slow." She walked alongside the three-story building from twenty yards out, pressing through brush and giving wide berth to palmetto clusters.

"Have the place to my own." She went around the rear of the building. Tapping in the memorized door code, she raised the rolling door to Molly's motorcycle shop a foot, dropped, and slid inside.

"Gee, April, didja pack a flashlight?" she chided herself.

In the dark, navigating was slowed to step by step. She passed through Allison's work area and Molly's cars. Her hand eventually brushed and grabbed the doorknob to Allison's studio apartment in the back-left corner.

"Allison," she called forward, hoping, but doubting he'd be allowed to live in the crime scene.

Silence followed.

She flipped on the light switch inside the door. There was his bed off to the side and the familiar, Spartan furnishings, reminding her of the couple of times she and Molly had hung with him here, talking crime schemes, unique printers for credit cards, and such. Searching his desk and drawers would be a waste of time. Even if he were foolish enough to leave out what she was looking for, the police would certainly have bagged them for evidence. She stepped into the kitchenette and unplugged his recharging hand lamp on top of the refrigerator.

"Where would he hide them?" She answered her own question by leaving the apartment and jogging up the stairs to Molly's loft.

It was clear that the police had searched the entire third floor. Tiny numbered evidence cones were set out, identifying where photographs were needed or where evidence had been collected. If anything, they had tidied up the usual chaos that Molly was comfortable with.

"Oh, Molly. Where are you? Are you okay?" She looked over her sister's clothing and bike parts, open wig case, and makeup boxes.

April stood in the middle of her sister's living area, hugging herself.

"This is making me very sad," she whispered to her sister's home and belongings. Wanting just to sit down and ponder, she instead shoved and turned to the couch. Prying up two rough plank boards and setting them aside, she reached down and typed in the combination to the safe.

With her new bank card and ID, April replaced the boards and repositioned the couch.

"Need to get my ass outta here."

She didn't move.

A minute later, she was lying down on Molly's bed. She breathed a trace of her sister's favorite perfume on the pillows.

"Gotta kill the hours until daylight." She pulled the blankets over her body, knowing sleep was unlikely.

"Shop for the new boat, one with improved internet and bigger fuel tanks... or?"

CHAPTER 31

Jr.'s Ghost

After the shooting, Rick Ables, Jr. blasted north for eighty
miles before driving east for two hours, finding a low-rent,
backwater town seven miles off the interstate. Scouting out
Tod's Motel, he liked what he found. The motel sat between a
shack and boat launch before a river, tall grasses hiding his
view of the water. Next door was a sleepy-looking gas station
offering bait and ice, the place looking as time-forgotten as
the motel. He parked the car in back, easing in between a six-
wheel work truck and an AC service van up on jacks.

He asked for a room for two nights with the side of his
face turned away from the life- stupid, sickly woman behind
the counter, paying with cash and making up a new license
plate number and make and model.

Eating from the vending machine beside the dead Free
Icebox, he otherwise kept to his motel room. Without
internet service, he watched the television news channels off
and on, learning little to nothing new. He did so sitting on the
front of the bed, using up dampened towels to press both

sides of the bullet hole in his side. The authorities were keeping it zipped as reporters speculated and pressed. The rest of the time, he slept.

———

Three days later, he drove a hundred miles northwest and steered into Big Deals Pre-Owned, a used car dealership in the seedy back streets of Jacksonville. The lot held rows of used cars in front of the mobile home of a sales office. Parking the Vette over by the shuttered service bay, he climbed out with his teeth clenched. His once nice and new shirt and pants were bloodied by the blackened bullet hole in the side of his belly.

Never minding his appearance, he was cheerfully welcomed by a saleswoman stepping away from her two forlorn peers. The nametag on her chest read, 'Miss Patty.'

"Welcome to Big Deals, honey. What would you like to drive away in today?"

"The dark blue Tauris."

"Yes, only one year old. Great car. Only two owners. There's also the 2016 Cadillac two-door. Get out on the open road in style. Fast and sleek. How much are we looking to spend?"

"I want the Taurus."

"Great! Have a seat in my office?" She gestured to a worn cubicle.

He negotiated the trade-in of the new and sexy Corvette for the beater, losing twenty grand on the deal.

"You're quite the bargainer," Miss Patty said, scribbling on the sales contract form. "With the, let me see, $9,356 credit, I can arrange for a detailing, service agreement, and—"

Rick Ables took out his Marshal's ID and lay it on the mess of papers on her desk.

"I want it in cash."

The badge flash helped a little. She agreed to the cash him out but insisted it be in the form of a check.

A painfully tedious hour later, he got the keys and drove off the lot in his new ride, a bland blue family car. His next stop was a grocery store branch of his bank. After paying off overdraft fees, he withdrew five hundred in twenty-dollar bills.

"Enough to carry me," he spoke to the car roof. "Confirm Molly's dead. Locate and end Cunt Two's miserable excuse of a life."

Negotiating the city streets back out to the coast, he drove south on A1A to south Flagler Beach, pulling into the Knight's Inn that offered, '$46 per night. Pool! Free Wi-Fi!'

He took a shower, still wearing his shirt and pants, most of the dried blood washing off and swirling in the pan.

"Looking good, handsome." He admired his face in the hand-wiped, misty mirror. His incoming beard was beginning to hide some of the scar with a black lawn of new growth.

Sitting in the room's only chair, he used towels soaked in warm tap water to dab and examine the bullet hole in his left side and the larger exit wound on his back. The round had missed organs and ribs but tore out a chunk of upper belly meat.

"Thank you." He closed his eyes as his ghost alighted onto his shoulder and spoke.

"What was that?" Rick Ables, Jr. asked.

"Oh, yes, good idea. Hit a Walmart for medical supplies and a new pair of slacks."

Getting out his laptop, he searched the local news stations for any updates on the shootings.

There was nothing but a rehashing of what he already knew. The identification of the third dead victim was still being kept from the public.

"What about that boat April was on?" He was nudged by the familiar voice.

"How would I find it?" He stared up into the popcorn ceiling.

His ghost shook its head like it was dealing with a retarded child.

"The police have security camera footage from that boat-yard if it exists," it explained. "Call them. Work your badge and smooth-talk for a peek."

Looking up the department's current-investigation phone number, he struck out, being fed to voicemail.

"Maybe there's some news footage of the boat?" his partner suggested.

"Thank you, let's look." Rick turned back to the laptop.

There was an unedited helicopter view of the crime scene on YouTube with the cameraman's narrative. No shots of the boat, and even if there were, they would be from above.

Next up, he watched the previous day's police news conference, hoping the boat might be shown or mentioned. No such luck.

The next video he watched was the archived local news channel's broadcast on the crime. WESH Channel 2's story opened with the tag team of an attractive man and woman introducing the story and footage.

Rick studied the entire six-minute broadcast before rewinding it. In the red banner embedded under the video, additional facts scrolled as he poised his finger on the mouse.

"There." He clicked and stopped the playback.

From the south on the river road, the cameraman had panned left to right from the river to the front of Klave's Boat Repair Shop and Storage.

He froze and copied the frame. The white boat was twenty yards out beyond the docks. Cunt Two and some guy were at the helm.

"Fuck. No name on the side of the boat."

Closing YouTube, he brought up the copied image.

His ghost spoke slowly, patiently, clearly about to lose its cool.

"What was that?" he asked his ghost, squinting at the picture.

"You heard me the first time."

"Yea, that might work. Thank you."

He scratched the boat's lengthy license number on the back of the hotel television station menu. Reading it back, he double-checked his accuracy against the stenciled ID running along the bow of the boat.

It took the next hour and a half to get on the path to the boat's ownership, starting with a search of the Florida Department of Regulations database of boat licenses. Further digging got him a phone number and home address.

Taking out his phone, he hit the owner's voicemail and left a message.

"This is Dan Block," he lied, smooth and confident. "US Marshal's Service. We need to talk to you about your yacht, the *She Got The Boat*. Call me immediately."

"Next?" he asked the ceiling and waited.

Nothing came.

He looked his hotel room over, noticing for the first time how small it appeared, little more than a box. Or a cage.

"Talk to me?" He closed his eyes.

In the following silence, he slid his chair to his right and looked into the mirror facing the bed. A frightening child-hood memory came to mind, the suspicion that the reflection was his true self, and he was the one trapped in the mirror.

"Am I here or in there?" He felt foolish asking but asked all the same, just in case.

He studied his unshaved long jaw and the gash with its stitching. Looking at his pale lips, he avoided eye contact.

"E-nough." He rode the chair back to the table. There was no more time for such nonsense.

Finding a pen, he wrote out a shopping list on the back of the television menu.

Thirty minutes later, he was in Walmart, shopping for the medical supplies followed by wheeling the cart through the Men's Department for a new pair of slacks and shoes. The ghost continued to ignore him.

"The hell with you." He got into line at the check-out, putting together his own plan. Staring at the back of the head of the woman in front of him, he spoke as the ideas came to him.

"A great big breakfast. Another shower. A few hours of bedtime."

The fat woman next in line turned her ugly face to the sound of his voice.

He ignored her, adding, "Then some nighttime hunting."

CHAPTER 32

April and Allison

April woke with a start, jerking upward and scanning Molly's loft. The first rays of sunlight were streaking in through the eastern windows.

"Damn, April," she chastised herself. "Should've never laid down. You just slept in a crime scene."

Using the phone on Allison's desk downstairs, she called for a taxi. After scanning the boatyard for a policeman or a sheriff, she let herself out quickly through the back door.

Hiking up the sand path that connected Molly's home to hers, she turned to the right on the road to the gate, never once glancing to the black rubble that had been her place.

She waited with her back to the gate to her and Molly's homes, keeping her eyes and thoughts forward.

The taxi driver pulled in twenty minutes later and drove her to the nearest 7-Eleven. She paid him and went inside to buy a burner. With the new cell phone taken out of its box, she crossed the road to the benches above the beach. The Flagler Beach pier was fifty yards to her left, reaching out into the swells and breaking waves. Tourists and surfers moved casually past her in both directions. Her first message was to Allison.

April: *You okay? Need a place to work from.*
　　Ali: *Good here. Glad to hear from you. Where are you?*
April: *South of the Flagler pier, staring at the sea.*
　　Ali: *On my way. You're being hunted. See you in fifteen.*

Allison parked down twenty yards from where April sat and climbed out of his old and faded two-seater Alpha. Sitting down beside her, he also studied the view.

Sensing him, April took his hand.

"Let's get you out of the heat." He stood and led her back across the road and up a block. He got the door to the Drunken Pelican, a dark, morning-drinker's bar, the carpet smelling of spilled beer and tobacco. They took a table in the back, its surface sticky from spilled drinks, and a newspaper sopping up some of the spills.

"Where are you living?" she asked.

"You'll laugh. I leased a mobile home."

"I like the idea of a *mobile* home, but really?"

"Betting I'll be long gone before hurricane season."

"Need a roommate?"

The female bartender called over at them, "No waitresses. Order here."

"Name your poison. If we order, she'll leave us alone." Allison stood.

"A Pepsi if they have it."

Returning to the table with two sodas, he saw April turning the page of the damp newspaper. He set the glasses down and slid the candle in a red globe closer for her.

"If you don't mind aluminum walls, you're welcome to the spare bedroom," he said.

April returned a warm and sincere smile.

"Molly's right, you're a love." She let her gaze linger a moment before looking back down at Sunday's advertisement section.

Allison sipped his Pepsi, admiring April's lovely face, even with her eyes tightened down and pondering, twisted lips.

"Oh, look. These are on sale." She swiveled the full-color advertisement for Ritchey's Buick GM dealership in Daytona. Her finger tapped the photograph under a list of features.

NEW 2018 Buick Enclave – Essence FWD
SALE PRICE $45,989
(MSRP $47,110)

"We could share my car," Allison suggested.

"If need be. Thank you, but I'm going to need more cargo space."

"Looks like a minivan with fat tires," Allison suggested.

"I agree. Says it's an SUV. *Enclave*. I like that."

With an hour to kill before the dealership opened, they took Allison's Alpha to the Oceanside sea-view restaurant for breakfast. At nine o'clock, they pulled into the new car lot.

A covey of sales agents watched their approach from the showroom steps. A rail-thin man in a blue and orange tie stepped forward, the first agent in queue.

"Fine day to drive away in a dream," he welcomed Allison before glancing at April.

"My name's Charles, but everyone goes with Chuck. Have an idea—"

"Hello, Chuck." April walked off to the three Buicks to her left. "We're liking the Enclaves."

"Excellent choice and we have a great selection."

Allison followed them to the vehicles. Chuck opened the driver's door and stepped back for April to admire.

She didn't sit but leaned in and examined the space behind the driver's seat.

"Got black?" she stepped back and asked Chuck.

"What? Yes. Twilight metallic."

"That's black?"

"Yes, of course."

"We'll take two."

Allison looked away grinning, loving April's seemingly random mind. Chuck's stammering voice added to the amusement.

"*Two*? Why, yes, I think... of course."

"You good at cutting through the bump and grind of add-ons and services?" April closed the car door.

"Yes, Ritchey's prides itself on getting our customers out on the beautiful Florida roads as quickly as... there's the necessary title and licensing paperwork. Shall we go into my office?"

"Let's."

Seated before Chuck and his barren desk with other salesmen's business cards in a tray, April took out her newly minted ID and debit card.

"We'll put them on this." She slid the debit card across to him.

Chuck set his pen down on the stack of documents and stared at the card.

"Of course. We do have several excellent financing—"

"On the card, please," April said firmly.

"Yes, not a problem." He sounded uncertain while returning to filling out the stack of forms.

April took Allison's hand and winked. Looking back to the salesman, she leaned forward.

"There's five hundred dollars for you if you'll get us around the two-hour dog-and-pony show."

"For a thousand, I can get you out of here in twenty-five minutes." Chuck began writing fast.

"You're a darling."

Leaving Chuck to the paperwork, April and Allison stepped out onto the showroom floor.

"What's the second car for?" Allison asked.

"Merry Christmas."

———

Standing between the two new twilight metallic Enclaves pulled around front, April typed a message into her phone and sent it to herself and Allison.

"Just sent you a list. If you're in, we each need to go shopping. Reply with your address, and let's meet up there?"

"I'm in."

Allison took out his cell phone and looked the list over:

April—laptops, wigs, makeup, and clothing.
  Allison—black market printers, groceries, guns, and ammunition.

"Will take all day, but I can get what you... what we need," he said.

———

Driving into the rundown west side of Daytona, April steered through block after block of flat- roof homes with brown lawns. A mile and a half in, the street dead-ended at the coquina wall surrounding the mobile home park. 'River View Estates' read the faded blue and white sign at the entrance.

After rolling slowly along the twisty and narrow lanes, she

found Allison's double-wide by the number on the curb. Allison's Alpha had been parked in the driveway by the dealership, leaving space for one more car. She parked like some of his neighbors did, on the yellowed Bermuda grass lawn.

Climbing out, she sat in the shade of the carport awning at the rust-pitted patio table. She killed the next hour and a half on her burner. There were four articles on the *Massacre in Ormond Beach*. Nothing new and still no details on the third unnamed victim. A press conference was scheduled for eight the next morning.

Her next search was for the details of the funeral services for David Klave and Molly's friend, Dennis. Before she learned anything, Allison's black Enclave backed into the driveway.

"You're fast," she offered. He was looking pleased.

"Favored by the gods." He opened the vehicle's rear door.

She walked down the driveway to help.

"I've got this," he said. "Get inside. Left the AC running."

April ignored him and gathered up a bubble-wrapped printer. Allison fished out his house key, set it on top of the printer, and gathered up several full plastic grocery bags.

It took them three trips to unload the car.

Allison carried the second printer inside, set it on the couch, and stood beside April.

"Charming place, no?"

"The AC is delightful. Furnished in 1980?"

"That's my guess." He joined her taking in the low budget and old and stale furniture.

"Is there actually a river view like the sign says?" she asked.

"Not that I've found. Sometimes I get the scent of brackish water when the wind's right. Your room is the first in the hall. More of a shoebox, I'm afraid."

"It'll be perfect. Thank you, Allison. For everything."

"It's okay if you go all gushy on me, but we have work to do."

"Yes, let's."

They shared a grin before braving the evening heat to unload April's car. That done, the two of them worked side by side converting his family room into what resembled a computer lab.

Allison started making their dinner as April sat at a table, pulling up Jr.'s bank account.

"He somehow got a lump of money, but he's not spending it," she told Allison.

"Where did he last surface?"

"Jacksonville."

"North of here but still in Florida."

"Yes. Think he is running?"

"If he's smart. Is he?"

"Jr.'s about half as smart as he thinks he is. I'll give him persistence and an oily black heart."

After dinner beside Allison on the couch, April went back to work while he cleaned up the plates and the kitchen. That done, he sat before his new laptop across from her.

"Working on?" he asked, studying his monitor.

"Looking for any news on the batch file I sent to the press and authorities."

"Explain?"

"Yes, I scattered all the grizzly details of Jr.'s antics. So far, not even a blip. You're working on?"

"New IDs for myself. Just in case."

As day turned to night, they worked silently, except for the occasional curse of frustration.

At midnight, he stood and stretched.

"Off to beddy-bye. You?"

"Sometime soon. It's been a long day."

Allison studied April's face in the blue and gray glow from her monitor, her thin fingers scratching a pen on a note pad.

"About Molly, I'm confident—" he started.

"Don't go there, please, can't afford that right now."

"Right. Quite the list." He noted the bulleted sentences.

"Yes, it's coming together. Go. Sleep."

"Yes, I'm on that." He leaned over, squinting toward the list. Across the top of the page, she had written in all caps

GIVE HIM SOME BAIT (ME)

CHAPTER 33

Gift From the Ghost

Rick Ables, Jr. woke from his nap with a groan, his deadened sleep interrupted by the vibrating of his cell phone on the nightstand. He lay completely still at first, groggy eyes to the ceiling.

Flipping through images of his torn dreams, he searched for a hint in each vignette he could remember, looking for contact, for a hint of divine inspiration. The only common thread was the color orange—the sun, the prison clothing, a pair of rubber jailhouse clogs.

"No." He groaned, fear filling his chest and twisting his belly in knots.

A flush of heat colored his face, and his body went slick with sweat. A rising gorge of panic forced him upright in the bed. Pulling his knees to his chest, he cupped them with his arms, never mind the stab of pain in his side.

Panting, he tried to still his breath and beat back the rarest of his emotions—doubt.

"Never." The image of himself returned from the dreams.

In sunset hues, his face appeared above the V-neck of an orange prison jumpsuit, a former US Marshal, tracker of escapees about to take up residence among those same vicious and vengeful captives.

"Run," came to him, and not from above.

"End the hunt and run for your life," he continued talking to himself out loud.

"North, then west for a few states. Spend a year under the radar. Come back for her then."

"It's not quitting," he argued, wiping perspiration from around his mouth.

"Self-preservation. You know some of the best hiding tactics."

Climbing out of bed, he scanned the room for his few belongings to be packed.

"Ohio? Middle of nowhere. Melt in. Get a job in night-time security?"

He placed his bloodied clothing in a plastic bag from a garbage can and put it by the door to toss into a dumpster. Pushing the medical supplies into his backpack, he patted his pockets to confirm he had his keys and wallet. That's when his cell phone purred.

Looking at it, he saw that a new message had come in from an unfamiliar number. He opened it.

The putrid fear and doubts dropped like a carcass onto the hotel room carpet.

"Where did my faith go?" He smiled, his facial stitches stretching as he read the text a second time. Looking first to his left shoulder and then the ceiling, he was chilled with gratitude.

"Gift from the ghost," he whispered reverently to his silent partner.

"Thank you."

CHAPTER 34

A New Start

With April working in the dining area, Allison cleared the coffee table for a workspace. Down the narrow hall, the window unit AC in his bedroom sounded like it was trying to eat itself. When the rattling circular noise started, Allison got up and closed the door which did little good because of the paper-thin walls of the mobile home.

"I'm gonna kill it. Okay with that?" April picked up the 9mm on the chair at her hip and stood.

"No gunfire, please. This is an upscale trailer park."

"Was kidding. How's it going?"

She sat back down at the table and returned to work, grousing at the persistent, irritating death throes of the machine.

"Ordered a new mold printer and most of the chemicals I'll need. Same with the micro-electronics. I'll need to go to Orlando for the two endoscopes. Black market. I'll buy the tools for all while I'm out."

"The brilliant Allison."

"Agreed. April? The skimming was Molly's expertise."

"Don't go there, please. Can't afford the weight and drag."

"Right, yes. How's the bait coming along?"

April hit Save on the document and looked over to Allison on the couch.

"It's close. Been through it three times. Tweaking for a balance. False flattery. A bit of seduction…"

"Mind if I toss my lunch now?"

"Not at all. I'm also giving him my regrets and an apology. And two hundred thousand."

"An apology, bit of the boobs and cash? Who wouldn't bite?"

"That's the slant."

"Read it to me?"

Rick,

What can I do to stop this?

What can I do to start to make this right?

We've both lost Molly. Isn't that enough?

Perhaps it is time to move on? Find a good and new life. New beginnings.

I'm so sorry our romance floundered. I'm to blame for that, and my heart is full of regrets. The chance for love was there, and I wrongly blew it.

Your hurt must be massive, and I'm to blame. Is there anything I can do to end your pain?

Talk this over with your Holy Spirit, and perhaps you can find it in your heart to forgive me?

At midnight, I'll be on the bench at the stairs to the Daytona pier.

I'm hoping you will come to me.

Let me tell you eye to eye how truly sorry I am.

Just me and a shopping bag with $200K, a small token to start my amends to you. Enough for a new start. Perhaps for both of us?

Sincerely,

April

CHAPTER 35

Molly

When Jr. entered the dark interior of Klave's boat repair floor, Molly was running. Two shots were fired, and she heard a pained moan turn into screaming out before her. Spotting Dennis, she turned to her left to him. He was inside the office at the desk, the bottom drawer open, David Klave's revolver in his hand.

"Give me that!" she screamed. The office window at her back exploded in a spray of shards.

Instead of giving her the gun, Dennis shoved her viciously, knocking her clean off her feet. The back of her head cracked on the concrete flooring. Momentary lights out, her vision was circled by red mist with streaks, the center a hazy black. Kneeling in front of her, Dennis fired two shots out through the office doorway.

When he was hit the first time, he arched back but stayed in front of Molly. Pulling the trigger over and over, Dennis was struck again and collapsed backward against her.

Molly didn't see Jr. get hit but heard his surprised, girlish scream of anguish.

Silence settled like dust, except for the yelling from out front.

She rolled Dennis's wet body off, both of them slippery slick with warm blood. Her vision blurred, the coordination of her arms and legs uncertain. She left the office and went deeper into the building. Climbing out a side window on the north side, she wobbled out into the thorn brush, cactus, and high weeds.

Heading out with no direction at first, she kept low, putting distance between herself and the building, fearfully listening for the sound of Jr. in pursuit.

A half mile out, she drew up and turned around. Hands on her knees, panting, she looked back over the terrain to the building. No sign of Jr. as best as she could see. She continued scanning for movement for two long minutes, her vision finally clearing all the way.

Surrounded by thickets, she collapsed onto her rear, facing a low, wild palm tree.

"Cracked my egg on the concrete," she said, ignoring the pain from the back of her head.

"He saved my life with his." She absently patted her bloody dress for bullet wounds.

"Klave. Dennis..."

Tears welled and fell, the anguish tearing at her heart.

After letting the pain and sorrow flame through herself for an endless few minutes, her eyes tightened down. Her vision blurred again by the tears, her lips pulled back from her teeth.

An icy knife of anger bordering on madness froze her sadness and regrets and shoved them aside.

She climbed to her feet, her balance wavering, her back to the south, and continued, walking slow. Her thoughts were still scrambled, and she couldn't yet begin to form a plan, and that was okay for the time being.

"Revenge," she repeated over and over through clenched teeth.

———

After turning to the west and reaching John Anderson Road, she walked a mile or so north. She broke into the first vacation rental she came upon. Upstairs in the kitchen, she drank handfuls of tap water. Putting in the drain plug, she filled the sink, pulled off her blood-stained dress and pressed it into the water.

Paying no mind to the bland vacation furnishings, she went to the south window and opened the blinds, letting in strong mid-day light. The glare off the glass stunned her eyes, and her knees faltered. Hands out for balance, she missed. Turning away, her next step felt foreign and distant.

"Fainting? Really?" she said softly before collapsing onto the tiles.

When she opened her eyes again, the first thing she saw was the light blue fabric of an unfamiliar couch. The light in the room suggested early evening. She lay completely still on the cool floor, her knees drawn up, her head pounding like a hammer.

"Naked?" she finally spoke, closing her eyes, fear rising.

"Did I drink again?"

"No." Swathes of memories of the attack and deaths swirled in her brain. Her hand went to the back into her wig, and she felt the swollen egg on the back of her head. Tracing it with tender fingertips, dried blood flaked off.

She worked her stiffened body upright. Her tummy clenched with hunger and thirst.

"How long was I out?" she breathed, climbing to her feet slowly.

"Quite a while," her hunger answered.

"Did I lose a day?" She couldn't believe so, but it seems likely.

"Possibly two?"

In the kitchen, she opened three cans of tuna with trembling fingers and ate as fast as possible, chasing the oily fish down with tap water. She consumed all three quickly, feeling her belly embrace the food. While her thoughts struggled to gather themselves together, she realized she was staring at the homeowner's two-shelf, well-stocked bar.

To distract herself, she pulled her dress from the bloody water in the sink and wrung it out. Carrying it to the big window, she laid it out in the fading light to dry. Flipping the light switch on the wall, she got what she expected. Nothing.

She found herself back in the kitchen without meaning to go there.

On those two shelves, there was a pair of full fifths of Bombay gin standing beside the others. She took one and sat down at the dining table with it.

"Power's out. No ice," she said, her thumbs and fingers rubbing.

The lust was running high.

"Concussion and alcohol, hmm... perfect deep blackout."

She had the place to herself, someone else's family room.

"Only lose the day and night. Then stop."

Slipping toward giving herself permission, she was seduced by memories of the initial, perfect lift and glide of intoxication, the release and smoothing of thoughts and feelings.

"Excuse me for a moment," she told the bottle on the table, trying to resist.

Hoping she could deny the urge to drink, she wandered

back through the house, borrowing a flashlight from a junk drawer. Checking out the garage downstairs, there was no car to borrow but a pair of old bicycles.

Back upstairs at the big window room, she looked down into the owner's small and moss- skimmed swimming pool.

She found herself seated again at the table with the bottle. The night's darkness was gathering.

Unscrewing the cap, she breathed in the liquor causing her mind to hover in a cloud of desire.

Two recurring passions swirled in the air before her.

One was revenge.

The second was getting erased with her table companion.

————

Climbing out of the owner's swimming pool, she gathered up her dress and pulled it on.

"That hurts." She touched the large bump on the back of her head.

Dripping wet, she put the full bottle of gin back with its mate on the shelf.

While swimming laps underwater a few minutes before, it had come to her that there was a phone call she had to make —to the police.

The kitchen phone still had dial tone. She called 9-1-1.

"This is Molly Danser, from the killings at Klave's Boat Repair. Please, please, please say I died. I promise I'll turn myself in soon. Please do this and give me a couple of days."

She hung up as the deputy on the line started asking what was surely the first of many questions.

Finding a pad of paper and a pen, she scribbled a note to the homeowners.

Thank you for having me. Lovely place. Great view. Might want to invest in a security system. I'll have a check sent over for the damaged door and the stolen bike.

Down in the garage, she wheeled a bicycle out through the side door. Pushing off and gliding, never minding the battered wrist cast, she steered down the driveway and turned in the direction of the coast.

"Oh, yes," she said to the glorious feel of handlebars again in her hands, no matter her unsettled sense of balance.

She pedaled up the street before turning north onto the walking path alongside A1A. To her right were the beaches under the roadside berm.

Thirty minutes later, she entered the coastal town of Flagler Beach. The pier reached out over the ocean to her right where small shops lined the west side of the road, each painted in the best of vibrant tropical colors. She rode across the small town's plaza in the glow of the decorative park lamps seeing a sign for coffee and donuts.

Ordering an iced mocha she really didn't want, she asked the sweetheart behind the cash register to use the house phone.

"Sure, if it's local," the middle-aged woman smiled, ignoring Molly's dirty wrist cast and crimson-stained wrinkled dress.

"It is. Can I run a tab? My friend will settle up."

"Sure, sweetie,"

She remembered Allison's often used phone number and dialed it.

"Hey, you, put April on," she said to Allison.

"Molly? Will wonders never... she's not here. Are you okay?"

"I'm fine."

"Where are you? I'll come right away."

"Flagler Beach. I'm at Swillerbees coffee shop."

"I'll be there as fast as I can."

Molly ordered a second iced drink and sat on the table before the coffee shop's front windows.

Forty-five minutes later, a pair of headlights blared against the coffee shop's front window, hurting Molly's head, but getting her up on her feet. Allison climbed out of an odd-shaped vehicle and greeted her with open arms and a hug.

"There we are." He held her close.

"My savior. Again." She pulled him closer, tighter.

It was Allison who broke their embrace after a minute. Taking a half step back, he took all of her in.

"You're looking rough."

"Thank you. Loan me a twenty?"

He fished into his wallet.

Returning to the shop, Molly handed the cashier the twenty, thanked her again, and went back out to the open passenger door of Allison's vehicle.

"It's great to see you again. Where have you been?" Allison asked.

"My bell got rung. Pretty sure I lost a day or two. What in the world are you driving?"

"April's doing. She bought each of us one of these."

Molly let it go. If her sister felt the need to buy a couple of Buick SUVs, there was surely a good reason. Pulling off her glued-on wig, she tossed it into the back seat. Placing her fingertips to the back of her head, she gently touched the fat swollen gash.

Taking Allison's sunglasses off the dash, she put them on.

"Ahh, much better. Tell me what's what."

"It's bad. He got away. So did April. They're looking for both of you."

Molly *saw* David Klave being hit and falling. Then

Dennis, bravely covering her and shooting back and dying on the office floor. She reheard the dying scream from a third employee deeper inside the boat shop. She had no idea why the authorities hadn't identified him but was relieved they hadn't. For all she knew, he was one of their own, working undercover.

"Taking me to her?"

"Exactly." He pushed the car up to seventy miles an hour through the two traffic lights of Flagler Beach and up to ninety for the coastal run up the A1A.

PART THREE

Now then, take your weapons, your quiver and your bow, and go out to the field and hunt game for me.

~ Genesis 27:3

CHAPTER 36

Benched

At eleven thirty that night, April parked her car in the empty sandlot back of the Daytona boardwalk and carried the heavy bag of cash across to the darkened sidewalk, passing along one of the many shops advertising *Three T's for $10*. The place was locked up and the lights off. Around the corner, she entered the plaza before the stairs to the pier, walking alongside a greasy spoon with faded photographs of food and pricing.

To her left, the boardwalk ran north with its shuttered arcades and shops. There was no one to see except a young woman working a trash spike, pulling a rolling garbage can. Waves were crashing along the beach, sending up low explosions on the flat, white sands. The bench at the base of the stairs was just outside the glow of a lamp post. Beyond the light, the pier reached out into the night.

She sat down, switched the 9mm safety off, and placed it under her thigh, the spare clip ready in her dress pocket.

Scanning in both directions, she set the bag of cash down to her right and walked through what was going to happen next.

"He'll be skittish. So, no sudden movements. Just me, sitting pretty. Put on a calm smile. Should settle him."

The minutes crept slowly, one after the other.

"Here's how this is going to happen," she spoke to herself again.

"Jr. will be holding the bag of cash.

"I'll slide the gun out while he takes a peek.

"First shot, for Molly.

"Second shot, for David Klave.

"Third shot, for Dennis and the other.

"Forth shot, for Molly again, to the face.

"Fifth shot, for me, straight to the heart."

Using the booms of the waves to help her count the minutes, she looked slowly left to right. The only movement was the girl with the rolling trash can moving away to her right.

Ten minutes passed.

"Come at me from behind?" There was nothing she could do about it, hoping to hear his shoes scratch on the sand on the beach steps.

Sensing midnight had come and gone, she fought the desire to take the 9mm in hand.

She stared into the two routes he'd have to take unless he was out on the sand, either along her same path or up the boardwalk from the north.

She killed two minutes looking inside the bag of bound fifty-dollar bills.

Breaking waves continued marking time.

"What are you up to?"

Sea mist began to bead on her hands and face.

Another two minutes passed.

Wiping the moist skim of faint dew from her lips and brow, she kept her eyes working for a sign of him.

"Did you run?" She thought about the certain shitstorm the batch files she had sent to the four corners created.

"There's nowhere to hide from that."

The two likely angles of his approach seemed to stare back at her.

A green golf cart appeared on the boardwalk from her far left. It was creeping along, its electric engine making a low whirr. She studied the distant windshield along with cautionary glances back to her left. No one in it except the driver that she could see. The person's body shape unclear.

When the cart was thirty yards off, it was all she could do not to slide out the gun.

"That you? Getting clever?"

The cart drew to a stop ten yards away.

The young woman she had seen earlier took the lid off a trashcan with a fresh plastic bag in her belt loop.

Five minutes later, the cart disappeared by turning left into the plaza.

The waves continued to crash.

April felt the tension beginning to sag.

She threw her shoulders back and sat up straight and alert.

"Show up now, you dog fuck."

CHAPTER 37

En Route

Rick Ables, Jr. left the motel with plenty of time for the meet-up but drove fast, nerves firing, and sweat oiling his face. He switched off the AC, hoping that would help the Taurus's engine run quicker. The headlights worked the vacant streets.

"Fuck the A1A." He jumped onto Highway 95 with its multiple lanes paralleling the slower coast road. The Taurus accelerated but complained with a wobble in the steering.

Wanting to run the car up to a hundred and see how much further it could do, he forced himself to remain in the middle lane.

"Last thing I need is, 'Hello, officer.'"

His cell phone's GPS led him onto the ramp to the Dixie Highway. He planted his foot deep into the accelerator for the next stretch of straightaway. The next turn put him on a ridiculously slow two-lane road.

He blasted the Taurus on every straightaway and got the tires screeching through every turn. Swamplands ran along his left, and a canal rode the shoulder, the water nearly as high as the pavement.

His GPS dumped him onto High Bridge Road, and he was forced to first let off the gas, then lock up the brakes, the car wanting to swing its tail out.

The drawbridge was up, lit with flashing lights under sodium lamps.

A sailboat was passing through at a leisurely pace.

"You fuck." He struck the dash with his fist.

The Taurus was stopped at an angle from the skid. Headlights pulled up from behind.

"Give me some help?" he asked his holy ghost. It came to right away. He watched the movie play—him sitting down beside April, nodding along to her blah blah blah, agreeing to whatever. The film ended with his blowing her brains out with two shots clinically aimed.

The passing sailboat was an agonizing slow twenty yards past the raised bridge before the first alarm rang.

It was another minute before the crossing bar in front of him raised, red light blinking, the alarm finally silent.

He started across, the tires echoing on the steel plates. Back on pavement, he gripped the wheel and spun the tires, looking into the next turn. That's when his mirrors and rear window filled with flashing blue and red lights.

Tempted to run, it was like another wiser hand tapped on the blinkers. He came off the accelerator and turned into the sandlot leading to the High Bridge fishing park. The two cars sat front to back.

Unlike Rick, the officer was in no hurry. He remained in his cruiser, chatting on his radio, likely running the Taurus's temporary plates. A handful of minutes passed before the male officer's voice called forward.

"Keep them on the wheel."

Rick did as instructed.

The officer appeared at his window three minutes later—buzz cut, tan, and handsome, mid-forties. Rick put on his best sheepish smile.

"License, registration, and proof of insurance."

Rick lifted his right hand and got the sale paperwork from the glovebox.

"Lost my wallet," he handed over the paperwork.

"How'd that happen?"

"If I knew, I would—"

"Where you headed tonight? Clocked you earlier running like a bat out of hell."

Before Rick could come up with a lie, the officer took his paperwork back to his cruiser.

Waiting until the officer closed his car door, Rick took his right hand off the wheel. He retrieved his backpack from the back seat. Shouldering it, he climbed out. Taking two steps toward the cruiser, he ignored the shouts and glare of the spotlight, and he turned at the back of his car. And ran.

Crossing the sandlot with the river to his right, he came to a wire fence twenty yards away. Clearing it, his wounded side screaming from the effort, he ran into the pines and hip grass. The officer was shouting at him to stop and yelling into his shoulder radio.

Rick splashed through a drainage ditch filled with foul backwater from the nearby river. His wound screaming at him to stop, he climbed up and out the other side. He tripped up, bit off the scream in his throat, gathered himself up, and continued running.

A half mile north, he came out of the trees and into the moonless night.

No longer hearing the officer and with no sweeping flashlight at his tail, he slowed, his hand pressing his injured side. In all directions, the terrain rose and fell across the sand mounds topped with sharp-edged foliage.

"Has my name on the paperwork," he pressed on, wishing he had thought to use an alias.

Out before him were endless miles of tall swamp grass, palmetto clusters, and sun-killed thickets. He turned in the direction of the river to his left where the tree line continued before a strand of skeletal oaks.

No longer running, he trudged a quarter mile until he was brushing hanging Spanish moss from his face as he walked through the trees.

Coming upon a forgotten one-lane road an hour later, he followed it. When it turned eastward in the general direction of the ocean, he stayed on the crumbling pavement until it became a sand road. A half mile in, the tree line up ahead was glowing from a white bulb hanging over a front yard.

He approached the isolated house slowly. Its windows were darkened, and a chicken wire fence extended out from both sides of the house like two sagging mesh wings. In the light of the lamp from above, sat an old and neglected Oldsmobile four-door, parked right up against the porch. Beside it was a pickup, easily fifty years old. The truck was rust-pitted, and its dented body rested over worn-out dirt tires.

The spare key was in the glovebox. The pickup looked like it had not been in a muffler shop for a few decades. Putting the column shifter in neutral, he pushed the vehicle out onto the road before climbing in behind the wheel. Pressing the spongy clutch pedal, he cranked the ignition, dropped the three-speed transmission into first, and drove away.

"Gotta find the A1A. Know the way from there."

He slid his hand inside his backpack on the litter-strewn bench seat, feeling for the hard shape of his gun.

"Only an hour and some late."

Eventually, a sand-washed turn dumped onto a two-lane,

and he could grab third gear. The yellowed headlights carved a tunnel through the hanging moss in the hundred-foot oaks.

"Look at my face," he chose the first line to say to April. "What you've done to it."

The last line came to him quickly.

"Now, I'll splatter yours."

He leaned out into the wind at his window and spoke to the black sky above.

"Get me to April on that bench. She'll wait. Has to wait for *me*."

CHAPTER 38

Reunion

Deeply suspicious, April left the bench with the bag of cash in one arm and the gun in her free hand. Her steps were slow and light. Looking in all directions for sudden movement, she rounded the corner of the t-shirt and tourist crap shop.

"Step out," she dared Jr., looking across the narrow street to the parking lot.

"Let's end your worthless life." She started across the sand to her car.

Headlights entered the street to her left, coming from the A1A intersection. They were running fast. Dropping to one knee, she set the bag aside and with the 9mm in both hands, sighted in on the windshield above the lights. The vehicle turned hard, tires screaming, and raced up the street toward her. Finger poised on the trigger, she tracked the car, ready to fire.

The car's brakes locked, and it leaned to the right as it bounded over the raised driveway and entered the parking lot.

The tires raised sand dust as the car raced across to hers parked before a street lamp. It scratched to a halt beside her identical-looking Enclave. Molly climbed out on the passenger's side, scanning the shadows outside the cone of light from above.

April dropped the gun into the cash sack and ran.

The bag of cash hit the sand at the back of the car just before April swept Molly up in an embrace.

"Molly, Molly," she chanted, her sister pulling her close.

"My crazy April," Molly half cried, half laughed.

April lifted her sister and swung her halfway around.

"I just knew." April released Molly to her feet. "This is brilliant!"

The two took hands, foreheads touching.

"How did you get away? No, that can wait. What's with your eyes?" April asked.

"Dunno, what's with my eyes?"

"Dilated like black moons."

"It's nothing. Got bonked on the head."

Allison climbed out of the second Buick and circled to the sisters.

"Lovely reunion. I'm getting all gushy, but we need to go."

Looking at the bag of cash, he asked April, "What happened?"

"Scumbag didn't show."

Allison opened the trunk and set the bag inside. "We should go." He was nervously scanning the late-night parking lot. The air was misty, not quite a fog. A spinning breeze was sweeping food wrappers and paper napkins this way and that.

"He's right." April finally let go of Molly, and the two got into the second car.

As Allison backed out, April put the vehicle in reverse and looked at Molly, then back over her shoulder.

"You okay?" April asked.

"I'm not right in the head." Molly smiled, liking the phrase.

"Never were."

"Me? You're the one driving a SUV."

"Don't laugh. They're practical." April followed Allison across the lot.

"And I'm the one got her head clocked."

The sisters bumped shoulders, and Molly took April's free hand.

The two vehicles formed a slow-rolling train through the dark streets of late-night Daytona. Allison led the way to the back streets. Fifteen minutes later, they passed the faded sign for the River View Estates.

"This is... *cozy*," was all Molly could find to say as they idled along the rows of mobile homes.

April parked on the lawn again, and the sisters walked across it to Allison holding the door open, the cash bag hanging from his arm.

"Are fuzzy slippers required here?" Molly winked at Allison, easing past.

Inside, she looked the furnishings over, biting her tongue before offering a sincere, "Thank you."

"Money was tight," Allison explained.

"Place is perfect. Mind if I take a shower?" she asked as he sat on the couch before his computer and printers.

Instead of exploring the tight hallway for the bathroom, she curled up on the couch, resting her head on Allison's thigh.

April opened her laptop at the kitchen table. "We need to regroup," she said, looking for a message from Jr. explaining his no show.

"Stub out his shit-filled life." She scrolled, seeing nothing.

"I wanna play, too. What was in the bag?" Molly closed her eyes and settled in.

"Cash," Allison answered.

"Bait," April corrected.

"I can almost see the hook stuck through his bony skull." Molly grinned.

"For starters, yes." April began typing a new message to Jr. Molly stretched her legs out and closed her eyes.

"Ali?" she said softly. "Are we going to miss the Santa Cruz 200?"

"We'll eventually get the bike and printers and all from Klave's."

"Let's focus on squashing Jr.," April said from the table.

"Right, yes. Sorry, I'm not right in the head," she repeated, smiling faintly at the phrase.

"He killed Klave, Dennis, and someone else." April typed a sentence, deleted it, and glared at her laptop monitor.

"I'm seeing a great big pink eraser for his worthless life." Molly raised her cast and extended her middle finger.

"Sleep, lovely." April paused and turned to her. "You're still not all right in the head."

"Okay if I kill you?"

The mobile home began to swelter like an empty pop can in the glaring hot August morning. Allison was still seated on the couch, head back, mouth open, sleeping. April was no longer at the table, having wandered off to her bedroom in the wee hours.

Molly sat up, blinking, hand to the injury on the back of her shaved head. Somewhere in the night, her wig had come off. The heat and light hurt. Her fingers absently tracing the shape of the swollen wound, she got to her feet slowly, her balance a bit woozy. She looked in on April, still asleep in the bunk-size bed down the hall.

In the kitchen, she stirred through the shopping bags on the counter, grinning for the first time that morning, pulling out a box of quick-mix pancake batter.

"Just add water," she read. "I can do that."

After starting a pot of coffee, she took out a skillet and stirred up a bowl of buttermilk pancake mix. Allison woke, looked across to her, and with a hand raised, mumbled, "Taking a shower."

Molly poured batter into the skillet and found a spatula. She was flipping the pancakes over when April wandered in, all crooked sleepy smile.

"There's my Molly."

"Love you. Find us some plates?"

The three ate breakfast, Allison and Molly on the couch, April at the table.

———

"You ever hear about jackpotting?" Allison asked Molly.

"Yes, I've looked into it but just the mechanics. I'd need Jeff the Prof for the software."

April looked up from the draft of the Jr. message on her laptop.

"Molly, okay if I kill you?" she asked.

"Sure, make it dramatic, please."

April added a few words.

"What do you have so far?" Molly asked.

Rick,

I waited and waited for you. I hope you are okay?

Molly interrupted, "I'm gonna yak."

"You should."

April continued reading.

I'm heartbroken. Just learned that Molly... died. She bravely clung to life but slipped away.
  I'm sorry for your loss and mine.
  I waited, hoping we could find a way, a solution.

I have your money. I hope you'll talk to me.
Can we try again? Same time, same place?

April

"Want anything changed?" April looked across to the couch.

Allison shook his head.

"How about 'stick your gun in your mouth and pull the trigger a few times'?" Molly suggested.

April nodded but didn't type. She hit Send.

Pushing back from the table, she left the laptop with the messaging program running. Going to the kitchen, she started washing their dishes in the sink.

"Seen my shoes?" Allison asked.

"Going somewhere?" Molly asked.

"April has a gun. I want one."

"Me, too."

"Of course." He found his shoes and car keys and left with a thousand from the bag of cash.

The dishes done, April filled a damp cloth with ice and sat with Molly, pressing it to the back of her head. They both looked across when the laptop pinged.

April went to the computer and read Jr.'s reply to Molly.

Flagler Beach, today at noon. Fifty yards north of the pier, right across from the
7-Eleven. Wear a swimsuit.

CHAPTER 40

"A Very Good Day"

Rick Ables, Jr. woke up lying on the bench seat, the door open, his lower legs dangling and numb. The old truck was parked back in the oaks and tall grass at the rear of Tomoka State Park. Sitting up slowly, he shook his legs to life, looking over the sandy campsite he had found the night before. Unlike the shadows and black foliage in the headlight beams, in the morning light he saw that he was surrounded by greens of every shade, including those of cash. He stared blankly for a minute before scooping his cell phone off the dash.

A message had come in. The number familiar. Standing on tingling legs, his side screamed at him after hours of being prone. The rear of the pickup was in the shade. He dropped the tailgate and sat down, opening the message.

"About what I expected," he spoke to an angular swatch of promising blue sky in the tree canopy.

He wiped sweat from the good side of his face. The sticky heat said it was going to be another maddening hot day.

His intended next message had come to him in his sleep.

Not as words to type, nor a movie, but a few snapshots—images of a time and place.

"It's going to be a very good day," he spoke to that same small view of heaven above.

"Gonna see Cunt Two fall. Just like Cunt One."

He repeated that, adding a bit of sing-song rhythm.

It only took him a minute to compose his reply and send it.

Flagler Beach, today at noon. Fifty yards north of the pier, right across from the
    7-Eleven. Wear a swimsuit.

"First things first, a big boy breakfast." He scooted off the tailgate and fished out the truck key. Rubbing sweat from both sides of his bearded, scarred face, he looked down at his filthy clothing.

"Then some shopping."

CHAPTER 41

All Dressed Up

"Noon on a beach?" April tilted her head at Molly.

"Daylight and crowds. He's almost showing some smarts."

"Dammit, didn't get a swimsuit." April crossed to the bags and boxes along the door wall from her shopping the day before. "I'll stop on the way."

The two kneeled and unpacked the wigs and makeup kit and clothing onto the floor.

"You shopped for both of us?" Molly looked to her sister, her hand and cast draped in a raven, face-cupping wig. "Not knowing."

"I knew."

Molly continued watching April, who was opening makeup compartments.

Sensing the look, April leaned and kissed Molly's cheek. "Don't get all gushy now. We've got a lot to do."

"Right." Molly looked up at the clock on the wall—8:17 a.m. She unpacked the last three wigs and slid a clothing bag over.

April was unpacking a portable skin spray kit beside a five-pack of different hues.

"Did you hit a Goodwill?" Molly asked.

"Bag at the end."

"I'm going with the Cocoa Love color." April slid the four remaining canisters to Molly.

Molly opened the Goodwill bag and pulled out a cheap striped blouse with a collar stain and a lime wool skirt.

"Crazy woman again?" April asked.

"Yes, I like her."

"Same." April put on her favorite wig, the blonde *JF*-stirred mess.

"You did well, sis." Molly reached into the bottom of the bag. "These are some fine shitty street shoes."

"Thank you. I'm thinking about how I'm going to do him."

"Me, too. I'll send Ali a text to hurry." April took out her phone.

"Odds on, he's going to want join in."

"I know. We'll keep him back. He'll need to drive when it's done."

"How do you see it?" Molly asked.

"I stroll up the beach, holding nothing but the bag of cash. He'll either wait or start toward me. At ten yards, I start firing."

"I like the idea of both of us shooting him."

"No." April's voice was resolute.

"No?"

"I want him to myself. His eyes to mine," April said.

"That's brave. And nuts. So, nope. You get within ten yards, and I'll come at him from the side. Both of us can empty a clip in him."

"Let me think on that."

———

A few minutes before eleven, Allison returned with two paper bags. Each held a Smith and Wesson with a full backup clip. He studied the girls in their new looks—Molly wearing a disheveled dress and bug-size ugly sunglasses, and April in her underwear, her arms and legs out, letting the last of her dark tan dry.

"You look like one of my crazy aunts," he told Molly.

"Put this on." She tossed him a mahogany page-cut wig.

"So, I have to be the creepy guy on the beach?" Allison tried it on.

April dropped her arms and kneeled before the paper bags.

"Couldn't get Glocks?" she asked.

"It was eight-thirty in the morning. I'm lucky I didn't get shot."

"They're fine. Thank you." April pulled on a beach dress, picked up the bag of cash, and led the way outside.

"My car?" Allison asked.

"We're taking two." April walked to the lawn. "I need to stop for a swimsuit. Gives Molly time to steal a shopping cart."

"That would be a nice touch." Allison opened the door for Molly.

"You're a love but shut up and drive."

On the way, Molly laid out for Allison what he was to do and what he wasn't.

"Here's how it'll happen," she told him. "April will walk up to him on the beach. I'll approach from his side. You keep the car running and be ready to hotfoot us out of there. You can get out but leave the car running. Keep the gun in your pocket. You're not gonna need it and don't want to be seen with it."

"That's all I do?"

"You've never done this," Molly said

"And you two have?"

"No."

"I don't come off as very brave in your plan."

"Right, but you *do* come off alive."

"That *is* good."

CHAPTER 42

Noon on the Beach

April parked in a church lot one block in from the beach, leaving the keys in the ignition and the doors unlocked. She carried the cash and her gun in the beach bag with handles she had bought along with the swimsuit she was wearing. Passing along a row of pastel-painted houses and shops, her first view of the ocean carried a faint breeze off the surf. She crossed the road on bare feet, the sidewalk on the other side cooled by a dusting of white sand.

Cars lined the beach walk. She wove around a young couple with a stroller and walked past a gaggle of surfers leaning against the hood of a car.

"Party with us?" one of them dared.

She ignored that, keeping her eyes forward, scanning.

Up ahead was a restaurant at the base of the pier, the Pelican something. Across from it was the 7-Eleven. A crowd stood around the restaurant's menu board, yakking back and forth.

At the top of the beach stairs just past the restaurant, she searched for her first glimpse of Jr. No luck with that, but she did pick out Molly fifty yards up the beach walk, leaning on the railing, talking loudly to herself, no one near her, looking down at the beach.

April descended the stairs to the pier out over the waves to her right. She stopped to let a family of pale-skinned tourists pass.

Walking along the water's edge where the sand was hard, her ankles being licked now and again, she searched for him. There were men surf fishing, their bodies nothing like his. Two elderly men were walking toward her, lost in their own animated conversation. Another man was twenty yards out, looking up the beach, trying to convince a woman of something. Still, another man was sitting on a white bucket beside two fishing poles planted in the sand. Further on, no single men. No sign of him.

Fifty yards along the shore, she stopped. A child yelped, and she spun around. The little boy was splashing with delight into the water.

"The hell are you?" She studied all movement back up the beach for him. Nothing.

She looked at the faces up above along the beach walk. He wasn't there.

She walked on, another slow and cautious fifty yards, reassured only by the handgun laying on top of the cash at her side.

Turning around, the distant pier reached out over the waves. Again scanning every male face she could see, she swore.

"Is this your fucking game?"

Eyeing the beach walk above and each and every man on the shore, she retraced her steps slowly, sweating by then, the August sun pressing down hard.

She was within earshot of Molly doing her ranting up at the railing when a voice growled at her.

"Park it."

His voice.

She turned her head slowly.

There he was. Stupid floppy hat, ice chest between him and his bucket and fishing poles, all in the shade of a beach umbrella, wearing a swimsuit and still in his brown socks and shoes. After waving her closer, he opened the cooler. She saw the gun on the ice. His hand took it up.

She sat on the sand. Bag of cash at her feet.

"No need for that." She glanced at the gun in his hand, then the ugly scar on his unshaven long face.

"Of course, I do. Slide the bag over."

She raised it into her lap instead.

"We're going to talk first," she said. "Mend some fences and all that."

"Actually, no, we're not."

"Let me get out my apology—"

"The fuck-ing mon-ey. *Now.*"

"You're being hunted. By everyone. I can help."

"There was a time your words..." He spit, the gun in his hand aiming at her face.

"Okay, Rick, okay. Let me have one packet, and I'm gone." She reached into the bag.

He leaned over to watch her hand.

She gripped the gun and fired, blowing out the side of the bag in his direction.

He screamed, hands going up, his left pulling the trigger.

April's pinky and ring finger dissolved in a spray of blood. She toppled on the sand, out in the sunlight.

He fired again, rising to his feet. Sand exploded in front of April's face.

She clambered up the beach a few yards before spinning

on her back, gun aimed. She pulled the trigger again and again.

Standing with wide-spaced shoes, he fired over the top of the umbrella.

April was hit again.

Another gun went off from up and above. Three fast shots. Somewhere else, Allison was yelling.

Rick's gun swept in that direction, and he fired off four shots. Bashing the umbrella aside, he was eye to eye with Molly.

He hesitated, his long jaw tightening. He swung his aim at her and got off two shots.

"Still can't get a woman done." Molly aimed at his face and emptied the gun.

———

Allison and Molly gathered up April and dragged her up the beach to the stairs. Allison cradled her up and headed for the car. People were screaming from all directions, ducking and running.

Molly got the door, and Allison poured April onto the back seat.

He put the Enclave in gear, his hands slick with his own and April's blood. Molly was slumped forward, head on the dash, her bloody hands splayed to the sides, moaning and panting.

He blasted up the road through two stops signs before turning west on the street with a Highway 95 sign. Behind, sirens were swirling and screaming toward the beach town from both directions. Foot to the floor, he tightened his slippery hands on the wheel, gasping, sucking in breaths.

April groaned.

Molly spun around.

"The money?" was the last thing she heard April say.

PART FOUR

"The higher we soar, the smaller we appear to those who cannot fly."

~ Friedrich Nietzsche

CHAPTER 43

Thieves

Allison struggled with April up into the mobile home, Molly getting the door, bent over, and dripping blood. He lowered her gently onto the couch and hobbled away for the bathroom and wet towels, a chunk of his calf missing. Sitting on the coffee table, he went to work first on binding the bloody side of April's head. The remains of her hand could wait until he stemmed some of the blood saturating her wig.

Molly had collapsed into a chair, a dishcloth pressed to her belly, the fabric quickly turning red.

"We need a doc," she said in Allison's direction.

"Yes, but first, all this bleeding..." He kept his focus on April. She was breathing, her eyes blank to the sky.

"Right. I'll call." Molly slid her burner cell phone from her pocket.

Allison removed April's wig with tender fingers and pressed a clean towel to the wound on her forehead. He kept the pressure steady until much of the bleeding slowed. He wrapped her head with a fresh towel. Going to work next on her hand, he used scissors to cut away two dangling flaps of skin where the two fingers had been. He cleaned the wound and wrapped it.

"Any luck?" he called over his shoulder.

"No, I'm trying my best. Who's your gun contact?"

Allison got his cell phone out and read her the number. Molly entered the number but didn't place the call.

"April?" She looked over to Allison.

"She's still with us."

"That's our April." Molly squeezed her eyes tight.

A moment later, she placed the call.

"Who's this?" A gruff voice picked up.

"You don't need my name, but I'm Allison's partner."

"So?"

"We need a doctor. Fast. The kind who doesn't talk."

"And?"

"That's all."

"And?"

"Right. How much you want?"

"Let's start with fifteen for me. You'll need to negotiate with the EMC."

"Deal," she told the man on the phone.

"Upfront. Cash. Let me give you the address."

"No. We're not traveling. You give me an account number, and I'll transfer it."

"Then, it's twenty for my trouble."

"We need the doc fast."

"Address?"

She gave the name of the trailer park and described the mobile home. "Baby shit yellow."

"You move the money. I'll make the call," the man insisted.

"No, you'll get the doc on the way, then I'll wire it. Text me your banking info."

"Twenty-five."

"No, you'll get the twenty."

Molly ended the call without waiting for his response. She stood up, and with her hands pressing her side, she crossed over to April. Leaning over, ignoring her sister's blank eyes, she kissed the top of the toweling on her head.

"You stay with us. We'll get through this. I promise."

She made her way up the short hall and ran the shower. Standing in the stream, she hiked her dress up to see and rinse the bullet hole in the side of her belly.

"Clean through," she said, her fingers touching the exit wound in her lower back.

————

Within the hour, a battered gray Pontiac pulled into the driveway and parked behind the tarp-covered Enclave. A young woman climbed out and rounded to the trunk, which held multiple case boxes of medical instruments and supplies. She left the trunk open after shouldering her triage backpack and taking out a support duffle.

She rapped hard on the door, shaking the aluminum.

Allison opened the door slowly, looking her over, up and down. After scanning the driveway and street, he stepped aside.

"Candy. For Candice. What have we got?" The young woman looked to Molly and then April on the couch. The EMC's body was the result of a gym life. Her skin was cocoa colored, her hair was short, straight and black, her eyes were serious and calm.

"Her, first." Molly pointed to her sister.

Candy looked at the gun in Molly's hand.

"Put that away. This ain't my first dance with criminals."

"We're thieves."

"The diff?"

"Move that stuff," Candy told Allison, pointing to the printers and equipment. When he had done so, she pulled the coffee table away and went to her knees before April. Looking her over, her hands opened the duffle bag at her side, and she made practiced choices, her eyes examining April's two wounds. The towels came off in the razor-sharp scissors, and she leaned in, penlight in her teeth.

"Her name?" she asked.

"April," Molly answered.

Allison sat on the floor at the side of Molly's chair. She took his hand. They watched on while the EMC talked to herself and the instruments in her hands.

"The money transferred," Allison said for something to say.

"Thank you." Molly nodded, leaning painfully to one side for a glimpse of April's face.

"April said there's enough money for three months," Allison went on, sounding distant.

Molly didn't reply, letting him babble if he needed to.

"We should get her to the hospital," Candy said, not turning around.

"That's not happening," Molly said.

"Thought so. Had to say it. You, the guy, go get the rest of my equipment from my car."

Allison stood and went out the front door.

———

Forty minutes later, Candy rose from her knees.

"Got her cleaned and drugged and stable."

"Thank you," Molly said, both she and Allison watching on, still side by side.

"Who's next?" Candy looked first to Allison's leg then the

blood-soaked towel Molly was pressing to the side of her belly.

"Her," Allison said.

"Your name?" she asked Molly.

"Molly."

"Okay, Molly, I need you to lie on the floor if you can."

Teeth clenched, Molly lay down after pulling her dress up to her chest.

Candy sat down next to her, legs crossed Indian style, penlight back in her teeth.

"Lots of gunfire. You guys win?" she asked, leaning over, both her hands inside her EMC bags.

Neither Molly nor Allison answered, both trying to look past Candy to April.

Candy went to work. After dabbing away the smeared blood, she poured a quart of antiseptic solution on the bullet hole.

With clean pads held to Molly's belly and lower back, she kept the pressure steady.

"Your eyes are off. I'll take your vitals later," she told Molly.

"My sister?"

"She has a forty percent chance. Let's get you and him treated, and I'll go back to work on her."

"Name's Allison," Allison shared.

Candy stayed focus on her craft, penlight then in her fingers, her eyes an inch from the blood-pulsing bullet hole in the side of Molly's stomach.

"There big money in what you do?" Her free hand went inside the duffle bag to her left.

Molly elevated her head and looked down her own body, to the side of Candy's face.

"Stay focused," she said, adding, "Please."

Candy put the light back in her mouth and filled a hypodermic from a small bottle.

"Look away." Candy gave Molly's wound the first of four treatments with the needle. Out of nowhere, she added, "Fuck sunburned Florida. Fuck the hubby and his low-flying schemes."

Allison wiped perspiration from Molly's brow.

"You three need at least a few days of care, especially April. I'm for hire if you can afford me."

"How much?" Allison asked.

"We'll talk later. It's not so much the money."

———

After Molly was triaged and mildly sedated, Candy examined, cleaned, and bandaged Allison's calf wound. Returning to April, she began running through her series of vitals tests.

"Looks like you three got the worst of it. Or was it just the first round?"

"We got the best of it." Molly's voice was firm and harsh, even with the sedation coursing through her body and mind.

Candy took out an electronic notepad and scribbled on it.

"Are you pros?" she asked over her shoulder. "Or this cluster hump your norm?"

"Fuck you," Molly's voice was garbled but strong. "Fix her. That's what you're hired for."

"I am. But... if there's big money and... *adventure*, I want in."

CHAPTER 44

Kill Men Jag

When evening turned into night, Allison uncovered the Enclave and drove it a safe distance south and inland. Wiping it for prints, he used a spray bottle of glass cleaner from the kitchen. Putting the key in the ignition, he climbed out and stripped off his clothing. They were stained from cleaning up April and Molly's blood in the passenger and rear seat of the SUV. The clothes and towels went into a garbage bag, which he set in Candy's back seat. She drove them to a dumpster behind a Gator-Jerky tourist trap just off a Highway 95 exit.

Back at the mobile home, Candy relieved Molly from the vigil with April. Looking for something to do, Allison went about moving and connecting his printers and laptop on the kitchen table, opposite of April's laptop and notepads. He didn't take the chair in front of his computer, instead going into the kitchen for a bucket of hot water and carpet-cleaner solution and a sponge.

"He'd make a good wife," Candy turned around and said to Molly, sitting in April's chair at the table.

"Your problem is? He's my partner," Molly fired back.

"No problem. Sorry. My mouth."

Allison began scrubbing at the blood-stains around the chair Molly had first sat in as well as the saturated carpet where she had laid when Candy examined and treated her.

Molly looked down at April's laptop. Opening the lid, she didn't start it but stared at the black screen, listening to Candy start a conversation on her cell phone.

"Hey, you, I won't be home tonight. Work."

Candy got an earful. Leaning away, the voice on the other end was garbled and hot.

"Cheez, I *am* working. When's the last time you pulled in a paycheck?"

More angry ranting. It went on for a minute, Candy cupping the phone in her cheek and shoulder. She was gently unwinding April's bandaged hand to clean and rewrap it.

"Next time you're up, stick your dick in the prop." She ended the call with her husband.

"Trouble in the nest?" Molly asked.

"You've no idea. He *was* a big shot pilot. Snorted that away. Does the same now with every buck he makes. Know what the soon-to-be ex does? One of his sidelines? See those banners advertising restaurants flying along the beach. Enough said on him."

"Sounds like he's expensive," Molly said.

Candy ignored the opportunity to vent some more. Finishing up with April's hand, she turned her attention to unwinding the head bandage.

"I'm starving," Candy said. "I'll cook. He cleans." She still hadn't said Allison's name since her arrival.

"His name is Allison."

"Know it. Sorry, got a temporary *kill-men* jag on."

Finishing up with April, she boiled up three boxes of macaroni and cheese. The three ate at the table, the printers and all blocking conversation. Dessert was another round of pain medication.

Starting April's laptop, Molly launched a search for news on the shooting. She found a local news station broadcast on YouTube, posted by the local FOX affiliate.

The lead-in showed the head and shoulders of two sad and serious actors in a news station, recalling the story. They added nothing new but did a fine job of cranking up the tension for viewers. The video switched to the interior of the police station. Five men stood before a cluster of microphones, the spokesman reading from a piece of paper, the other four looking on, grim and resolved.

Molly learned that the unnamed deceased—Jr.—was known to the authorities as part of an ongoing investigation. April's car had been located and impounded. The descriptions of the suspects were conflicted. April's spent 9mm and the bag of cash had been confiscated.

The video ended with the spokesman turning away and leading the other four stern-faced authorities from the podium of microphones, questions from the gallery being called out and not responded to. The reporters fired their questions, anyway.

"Witnesses saw others firing, have you found them?"

"Is this related to the Klave boatyard shootings?"

The video returned to the newsroom where the handsome male newscaster looked straight into the lens.

"Stay tuned, more to come."

The woman at his side at the desk was looking pained and caring.

At midnight, Candy cleaned and re-bandaged Molly's side and Allison's leg. She went out to her car and came back a minute later.

"I'm off to the all-night pharmacy. Running low on everything."

"How much you need?

"Five, six hundred." Candy looked at the list she had drawn up.

"How much cash we have here?" Molly asked Allison.

"We're running low," Allison said, taking out his wallet.

Molly studied Candy's neutral, tired expression. Candy used an impatient puff of breath to raise a curl of her hair.

"Let her have the bank card," Molly said.

"Chill. I'll be back. Gonna pull her through," Candy said at the door, looking to April laying on the couch with her IV drip, monitoring equipment, and sensor wires.

Allison put his arm around Molly and led her to a kitchen table chair.

"Where to? And how?" Allison asked, sitting down beside her.

"A hungry pilot?" Molly said, looking deep into Allison's eyes.

CHAPTER 45

Candy

Molly slept on the floor at April's side. She woke and watched over her sister, whispering to her.

"Stay with us." She adjusted the blanket upward under April's chin, careful not to bump the monitoring pads and wires and IV lines.

"Come back to me, my darling one."

April's beauty was still there, no matter the swollen and bound ruination of her forehead. Molly reached across and took her hand, her thumb gently massaging April's palm.

"You and I, we're not done. No way."

April's gaze was off to a million miles away. Her slight breathing was reassuring as was the warmth of her hand.

"Your job now..." Molly rose from her knees and kissed April's cheek, "... is to hold on."

Molly stood up, reluctant to leave her sister, and checked to see that Candy was still with them. She found her sleeping in April's bedroom.

She brewed a pot of strong coffee, flavoring the trailer

with the dark aroma. With her first sip, she washed down a spill of pain pills in her hand.

Candy wandered in, hair and clothing amiss, and poured herself a cup. She carried it to April, and after looking her over, reviewed the electronic readings.

"How is she?" Molly joined her.

"She needs time and real equipment. A hospital. Surgery, for sure. You, too. Pretty clear none of your organs were hit, but..."

"I'm getting ideas," Molly said. "We're going to need buckets of money to get us right."

Molly went and sat down before April's laptop. After seeing the hold still in place on their bank account, she got into her sister's TOR encrypted ransom messages and notes.

Reading the last reply from one of April's *clients*, she sat back and pondered for no longer than a minute. The billboard attorney had pushed back with an offered cut in the ransom amount to be wired immediately upon acceptance. She typed fast.

Molly: *Agreed. Send the money now, and I'll be nothing more than a past nightmare.*

She left the table and went and kneeled before April.

"And?" she asked Candy for a status.

"Like I said, she needs time and real equipment. A hospital."

"Can we move her?"

"We *have* to move her. She needs a clean and sanitary environment. Not this dump."

Molly returned to April's laptop and started down a rabbit trail of internet searches.

She stopped only once during the next hour to eat another round of pain meds. Allison wandered out, red-eyed, aiming for the coffee pot. He sat down Indian style at Candy's side, sipping from his cup, looking to April's eyes and slackened expression.

Candy took her cell phone from her shirt pocket and placed a call to her employer. She begged off the schedule for the next two days. With that squared away, she placed a second call to her husband.

"Of course, I didn't. The hell you thinking?" she said to his greeting.

Thirty seconds later, she cut off his ranting.

"Making money. You?"

That set him off again. Candy held the phone away from her ear, shaking her head. Molly watched on while standing from the kitchen table. She crossed the room.

"Give me that." Molly put her hand out for Candy's cell phone. Candy's eyes widened, but she relented.

"Your name?" Molly asked.

"Ryan, who's this?"

"Ryan, the pilot, listen. No questions unless I ask them. Can you fly planes larger than a puddle skipper?"

"Yes, but what do you—"

"You forget the rules. Want to make a shitload of quick cash?"

"Well, sure. I mean... who are you?"

"Enough money to save your marriage or fund a divorce?"

There was a pause.

"Is Candy listening?" he asked.

"You're not too swift with instructions. There are three of us that need to get far out of the area."

"How far?"

"I'll let you have that one question. Out of the country. I'm guessing one day's work for you."

"How much?"

Molly's teeth locked, holding her back from biting his head off for asking yet another question.

"My partner is going to give you our address," she measured out, handing the phone to Allison.

After giving the husband the address, Allison said, "He wants to talk to you again."

"Hang it up. Got nothing to add."

"She's not big on being questioned, mate," Allison said politely and ended the call.

Molly returned to the computer on the kitchen table. When Allison joined her, looking down over her shoulder, she was clicking through the sidebar of a menu of services for a town with pretty pictures—a stone village with green fields in the background.

"You're now in charge of these." Molly handed Allison her bottles of pain meds. "I'm liking them too much."

"Got it." He pocketed the bottles. "Where's that?"

"Port aux Basques."

"Never heard of it."

"Exactly."

A cell phone began to rattle and purr. They both looked to the bowl on the table where April's keys and phone lay. Molly reached over and picked it up. The call was from their local area code. Number unknown.

"Ali, go look out front." Molly watched on as the call rolled to voicemail in the display.

"Sure, what for?"

"Police."

Allison looked out the curtains of all the front room windows before heading back through the mobile home.

"Candy, come here, please."

"Whatcha need?"

"Dial your husband for me."

"Nothing!" Allison called from one of the back bedrooms.

Candy dialed and handed the phone to Molly. He picked up on the fourth ring.

"Change in plans," she told him. "What kind of car you got?"

"Suburban. What's changed?"

"Drop everything. Get here now. *No more questions.*"

He was still talking when Molly ended the call. She rose and carried April's phone into the kitchen.

"Quiet," Allison called out, coming back up the hall. From some distance, there was the *thut, thut, thut* of a helicopter.

Molly centered April's phone on a chopping block and took out a meat tenderizing mallet. She poised to pulverize it.

"Don't," Candy grabbed her arm. She nudged Molly aside.

The aluminum walls of the double-wide began to vibrate. The helicopter was surely within a few hundred yards.

Using a roll of tape from a kitchen drawer, Candy taped the phone to the cutting board, winding it twice. She left the mobile home at a run.

CHAPTER 46

All Sails Unfurled

April's phone sailed away along the Halifax River, hopefully clearing the inlet and starting a sea cruise in the Gulf Stream. Wherever it was headed, the helicopter would follow. It would be plucked out and examined. Messages would be read and numbers captured. The link to Jr. was on it and nothing more.

When Candy's husband arrived, she went out front and shouted to him to turn around and back it in. He obeyed, no questions asked. Inside the mobile home, Molly put April and Allison's laptops in a canvas grocery bag as Candy and Allison figured out how to move April. He carried her in his arms out to the Suburban with Candy at his side with the IV stand and bagged medical equipment. Working closely, the two of them laid her across the back seat.

"You ride with her," Candy told him, "Just squat on the floorboards."

Allison climbed in, and Candy closed the doors.

"Gimme those." She put her hands out to Ryan for the keys. "I'm driving. Know these back streets."

Ryan grumbled and obeyed. Molly nudged him aside and climbed into the shotgun seat. He climbed into the far back seat.

"Which airport?" Candy put the vehicle in gear.

"Ormond Municipal. East of 95."

"Know where it is, but... thanks."

For the next ten minutes, Candy navigated the back streets, an endless series of squared-off residential blocks with constant stop signs. She drove slow and steady.

Six miles from the mobile home in the middle of a sleepy row of track homes, Candy brought the Suburban to a halt.

"What the hell you doing?" Molly looked over.

Candy buttoned down all the windows.

"Listening for the copter."

Hearing only a distant hum of a lawnmower, she put the vehicle back in gear.

The neighborhoods were replaced by strands of forlorn stores and shops and used car dealerships. Out on one of the lesser avenues, they rolled past a police cruiser pulled onto the grass shoulder, the officer working paperwork on a clipboard.

"A really good sign," Candy observed, taking the very next left, then a series of rights and lefts.

In the far back of the Suburban, Ryan, the husband and pilot, was on his phone. He had rented the airplane and was working a buddy in flight control, filing a bogus flight plan.

While they passed through the shade of the Interstate 95 bridge, he called forward, "All set. Fuck, I'm good."

Candy and Molly exchanged a wordless look.

A mile from the airport, they passed another officer, this one in a sheriff's truck, sitting at an intersection, blinker running. No red or blues on.

"It's a tie-up, north of the terminal, space thirty-seven," Ryan called to Candy.

"Got it." She drove past the entrance to the run of tall fencing that led to an unmanned gate. Having been along on many flights with her husband, Candy drove past the T-hangars to the row of airplanes tied down on the tarmac.

She parked the Suburban alongside a twin-prop Piper Seneca, some guy rolling toward them in a golf cart. While Ryan and the guy talked, and he took the clipboard and keys, Allison and Molly waited at the open doors of the Suburban. When the cart drove away, Molly stepped to the open door of the Piper.

"I asked for a cargo area." She looked in on the row of seats.

"It's the best I could do. The seats collapse."

"Okay. We can make this work."

Within minutes, April was resting in the back area of the airplane, all her IV feeds checked, and the equipment running. Upfront, Ryan ran through his pre-flight with Allison at his side. Putting on headphones so he could listen in, Allison set the bag of laptops and handguns at his feet. Ten minutes later, they were in queue for departure at the end of the runway, the twin propellers blurring the wind and view as they waited for their turn in line.

CHAPTER 47

Newfoundland

Thirteen hours later, Ryan landed the twin-engine airplane at Deer Lake Airport on the island of Newfoundland. The Canadian province was a triangular-shaped rock surrounded by the icy gray seas of the Atlantic.

Having figured out the radio, Molly had called forward for a non-emergency medical transport. A Mercedes cargo van rolled up to the side of the airplane as Ryan braked at the refueling station. He was talking with the tower, explaining that he was flying solo and refueling only.

"I called for the medical guys because I've got the stomach flu," he explained to the other man.

The tower was more concerned with his flight plans. He began a word dance to stall while Candy and the two EMCs placed April on a portable gurney and extracted her from the plane in the shade of the wing. Molly and Allison climbed out and stayed out of the way.

"Please hurry," Molly said.

With April secured inside the van and under the care of

the second EMC, Ryan used Molly's debit card to refuel, Candy at his side.

"Where are we transporting her to?" the driver asked Molly, who gave him the address for the house she had found online and booked. She and Allison climbed inside.

"Candy, let's go," she called through the sliding door.

"This looks illegal," the driver told Molly before climbing in behind the wheel.

"It is. And it pays well. You game?"

He climbed in and started the engine.

"Candy," Molly called out.

Candy ended her strident argument with Ryan with an upward fling of her hand. She squeezed into the van at April's legs, and Molly slammed the door. Minutes later, Ryan capped the fuel tanks and with more lies and dusting of information to the tower, rolled the plane out and flew away forever from Candy's life.

"*I got this*," Candy growled at the EMC trying to help with April. He studied her expert handling of the monitoring pads and went around to the front of the van.

Kneeling at the back of two EMCs, Molly put her hand out to the guy when he took the passenger seat.

"Thank you. Your name?"

"Patrick. And you are?"

Instead of answering, Molly took the offered hand and did a quick study. Patrick's face was puffy from lack of sleep. His clothes and posture were slack, and the vibe said, *Married and stressed. If he were a car, it would be a worn-out minivan.*

"I'm Lans," the driver said, an Asian man in his middle fifties. His face was as pale and smooth as a headstone, only his eyes active—two black almonds watching the tarmac out front for the gate.

"Welcome to the Land of the Fish," he said over his shoulder.

"Also known as the Rock," Patrick added, slumping in his seat.

They passed through the unguarded gate to the aerodrome section of the Deer Lake Airport, Lans steering into the vacant surface streets of warehouses and flight-supply shops. Two miles of back roads later, he brought the van to a stop in the gas station parking lot before the entrance to the Trans-Canada Highway.

"What's up?" Molly leaned forward.

"We need to talk about money."

"Yes, that, of course."

"It's roughly a three-and-half-hour drive, two hundred and forty kilometers to Port aux Basques."

"Give me a number."

"I'm thinking two thousand, US."

"Done. We're strapped for cash. Give me your credit card, and I'll do a wire."

"I'll take cash."

"Fine. Find us an ATM."

"I'll want cash, too," Patrick chimed. "Two thousand."

Lans pointed over to the quick market back of the gas pumps.

Molly climbed out and with eight transactions, pulled out four thousand dollars. As the last spray of bills fluttered into the plastic tray, she spoke to the ATM.

"I'll see you later. You'll spill your guts."

Back inside the transport van, she handed over the cash and watched on as Lans drove out of the lot and up to the highway entrance.

"Why are we headed North? Isn't the Port in the south?" Molly asked when he steered onto the first ramp.

"Look out back."

Fifty yards back in the mid-morning fog, there was a white and blue police car. So far, no spinning lights. There was a sedan between them. Lans ran the van up to speed, staying just under the speed limit in the slow lane. The police cruiser was following, still no swinging lights.

Allison had his face to the rear window.

"He's on his mic."

A mile up, Lans put on the blinkers for the next off-ramp.

"Might be able to lose him in the tight streets," he said, studying the rearview mirror.

Molly looked forward. From what she could see, the approaching area they were headed for was a neighborhood of row houses and rocky hills.

The lights on the roof of the police car lit up. It roared into life, accelerating.

Lans restrained himself from mashing the accelerator.

They ran down the off-ramp with the cruiser closing in.

"Lose him," Molly pressed, gripping Lans' shoulder.

They came up to the stop sign. He turned to the right, and they started up a hill of square and sleepy residences. He blinkered for the first street to the right, a one-lane a little wider than an alleyway.

Sirens swirling, red and blue lights sweeping, the police car blew by, the officer mouthing into his microphone, looking straight ahead.

Lans navigated up the tight street, the bricks inches from taking off the side mirrors.

"Lucky us," Allison called forward.

"We need it, yes," Molly replied over her shoulder, eyes to the approaching side street. Lans was still determined to keep using his blinkers and roll slow.

A few minutes later, they were back on the Trans-Canada, heading south for their three- hour drive.

Past the edge of Deer Lake, the countryside rolled out in rough lands of green fields and gray stones. An hour along, the fog burned off, revealing little more but the same terrain along both sides of the highway—fields of green hay and rolling hills, cattle in pastures bordered with outcroppings of the gray rock, and from time to time, there was a low, wide stream of slow waters.

Two and a half hours later, they entered Port aux Basques from the north, the port on the southernmost tip of the island. With the address entered into the dash GPS, Lans navigated the sleepy roads to their rented house on Charles Street. He pulled into the driveway of the two-story box house like all the others on the block. It had been listed as a furnished chalet.

Molly climbed out, coded open the lockbox, and went in through the front. A minute later, the garage door rose. She stood to the side, chilled by the forty-degree temperature. Lans steered the van inside, and she tapped the electric switch to close the door.

Lans and Patrick transferred April inside, Candy guiding at the front of the gurney.

"Not in a bedroom," Molly instructed. "I want her in sight. The couch for now."

"I'll go break down a bed." Allison headed upstairs.

With April laid out and monitors and IVs running, Molly followed the two EMCs out to the garage.

"Thank you," she told each with a shake of their hands.

"Get her to a hospital." Lans kept his eyes locked on hers until she nodded.

She buttoned the garage door down as they drove off into the early afternoon.

Back inside the main room, Candy was on her phone. She covered the mouthpiece when Molly entered.

"I'm on hold for the hospital admin. Going to convince them to admit without the usual paperwork and questions."

Allison was building the queen-size bed five feet back of the fireplace. The window to his right revealed their large backyard of green grasses. A few minutes later, he and Molly had April moved up onto the bed and covered with sheets and heavy blankets.

"We're to bring her in at the start of the four to midnight shift," Candy said. "Discretion promised."

Molly sat down at the dining table with a pad of paper and pen from a kitchen drawer. The first item on the list—

---*Warm clothing for everyone.*

The next line—

---*Groceries.*

She took a break after listing a dozen items. Candy had touched her shoulder.

"Go shower. Then I'm treating your wound."

While Molly showered, Candy unwound the bandage on Allison's calf and cleaned and bandaged it with antiseptic pads.

"Having a rental car delivered," he told Molly, pocketing his phone when she came back into the room.

Standing at the table, Molly kept silent as best she could while Candy inserted an ointment-soaked Q-tip inside the bullet hole in her side.

"You can yell," Candy told her.

"I'm good. Just finish. Fast." Molly panted, her hands gripping the table for balance, her head light and swimming from the pain.

Candy used a second Q-tip to clean up the exit hole in Molly's back. When it was two inches in, Molly screamed.

Candy finished up as quickly as possible but not before she had thoroughly treated the injury.

"Pain meds. Now," Molly told Allison, her face flush, her skin beaded. "Make it a double."

Unable to sit, she carried her pen and paper to the fireplace. Allison helped her lay down and stretch out before getting her the pills and a glass of water.

She lay still for a few minutes until her breathing normalized and most of the pain receded. Candy took to April's side, pulling over a chair and holding her half-ruined hand.

"Make a list of what you need," Molly told Allison, who opened his phone to do so.

To her own list, she added,

---*Complete ransom negotiations.*
   ---*Make sure our trail is still dusted.*
   ---*April—best help possible.*

She wrote the final item in all caps and underlined the words.

---*MAKE MONEY.*

The Three Bears and Goldilocks

Four months later...

Candy resigned from her day shift position at the 24-hour ER at the Legro Health Centre. Working there had allowed her to see to April daily and Molly and Allison, who had the evening and night watches. It was also a good opportunity to *borrow* supplies and medication for Allison and Molly, who were mostly all healed up.

That same day, April was released. Molly had paid the two EMCs, Lans and Patrick, for a discreet transport of her sister to the waiting private jet she had also hired.

April's gurney was gently lifted into the aircraft with Candy at her side and Molly following.

"You come back to us." Molly kissed April's check, standing to leave the airplane.

April was slack mouthed and situated comfortably, eyes unblinking to the curved airplane ceiling.

Molly took Candy in her arms and hugged her close.

"Thank you, thank you," she said. "Whatever you two need, don't hesitate."

"Will do. She's going to get there."

Molly kissed Candy's temple, both hands cupping her head. The jet engines started up, and Molly went down the steps.

She and Allison stood side by side on the tarmac before the Deer Lake Airport, their hands joined. Both wore parkas and boots, and their eyes remained on the jet as it rolled out. They were still standing in the frosted air as the airplane flew up into the clouds on its way back south to the States.

"You bring her back to me," Molly told the empty sky.

———

After the three-hour drive back to the chalet, Molly and Allison went to their separate bedrooms to pack up their clothes and met up again in the front room. Molly sat on the couch while he added the last bits of skimmer molds to the flames, sending up a stench of bubbling plastics.

"Closed on the sale of April's home and Klave's boatyard," she said, her laptop open on her thighs. "Have you seen her new place?"

"Show me." He sat down beside her.

"Whatcha think?" She showed the picture to Allison.

Allison smiled. A clean and furnished beachfront property with windows full of ocean view, located a mile south of St. Augustine.

"She's going to love the light, the view."

Molly let her smile linger a moment before tapping the keyboard and bringing up a saved search of links to news on the Rick Ables, Jr. murder.

She had tried and failed many times to befriend and buy off an inside source in the police department.

"The latest?" he asked.

"According to the press, the investigation has stalled out if you buy that."

"Where do you think it is?"

"In their teeth like a bone they won't give up. Every day they *don't* have a press release or news conference, I worry all the more."

Allison took up the envelope on the coffee table laying under the rental car keys.

"More dusting of the tracks," he said, taking out his and her new papers and passports.

"You're a wonder. Thank you." Molly opened her passport to the photo page.

"I agree." Allison smiled.

"Mary Brown?" Molly read. "How boring."

"Exactly. Come, we've got an ocean to cross."

Molly closed the laptop, pocketed the documents, and stood. She turned away from their living room for the past many months without a thought.

Allison closed the front door and walked down the driveway to the passenger side of the rental car. Climbing in, he looked to beautiful Molly in her new look for travel— leather boots and pants, worn-out gold t-shirt inside her black jacket, her wig a fiery short cut of redwood hues.

He took one last glance at the house.

"We were like the three bears and Goldilocks."

PART FIVE

Justice is truth in action.

~ Benjamin Disraeli

CHAPTER 49

Isle of Man

Allison waited for Molly behind the wheel, scanning the foggy streets of the village of Onchan. It was coming up on four in the morning. Molly had been at work for twenty minutes, five more than planned. Though practiced with the modified endoscope, finding the port inside the Diebold Nixdorf ATM called for surgical precision.

He scanned the street again, up and down the Village Walk outdoor mall. Not a light or soul to be seen. The ATM was recessed in an alcove between a gift shop and a florist boutique. Molly was on her knees before it, a penlight shining from the band on her head.

Though she had instructed him to remain in the rental car, engine running, ready for an escape, he climbed out to open the back door. She was crossing the road pulling two duffle bags on casters, both filled to the brim with bills of pound sterling.

Together they hefted the bags inside, and Molly joined him in the front seats. Allison put the car in gear and drove away, painfully slow and casual. If they got away, Molly had pulled off their very first jackpotting.

"Oh... *yes*." Molly drummed her hands on the dash in rare delight.

"Brilliant, you. Well done." Allison grinned, keeping his eyes on the road.

"With the last ransom and this, we're *in the money*." She actually sang the last part. "Now get us home. I want a one-hour workout, then blessed sleep."

Their lodgings were four miles off in the capital city of Douglas on the east coast of the Isle of Man. They had rented a loft over an enclosed garage.

"Sleep, yes. We've got ourselves quite a day later." Allison crept the car along at the posted speed limits, the headlights casting channels in the fog.

With the car garaged and the two duffels carried upstairs, Molly headed off for the spare bedroom they had outfitted with gym equipment for her.

Allison took the chair before the two canvas bags. He watched her walk away, all amazing hips and legs, her fiery wig bouncing. As she disappeared in through the first door in the hall, he closed his eyes.

"If only..." he said.

For a distraction, he unzipped the left side duffle. There was the mound of cash in different denominations, obscenely more than they would need for the next two weeks of the event, including the new bike and parts and the rent on the shop down by the track. He found a smile, wane and tired, and stood up.

"A shower. And escape into sleep." He went up the short hall to the bath in his back bedroom.

Fifty weeks a year, the Isle of Man was a laconic land of green fields, most spotted with lamb and cattle, the towns and villages often chilled by rains. People went about their lives at a steady, slow pace as those before them had done for decades, for centuries.

That all changed toward the end of May as preparations for the Isle of Man TT event accelerated. The ferries and airports delivered crowds of fans and race teams, and the streets filled with lorries and team trailers, leased taxis and rental cars.

A steadily increasing migration crossed the Irish Sea, many from the UK, but also a large contingent of international fans and press.

The streets teamed with foot and motorbike traffic, the shop owners and vendors happily greeting the many fans with flush wallets of vacation funds. The hotels and rooms were booked months in advance, the only vacancies, perhaps a spare bedroom, could be had if the late arrival had enough cash.

Banners, buntings, and flags of all colors went up as did the volume of music from all corners. A festival was kicking off, a celebration of motorcycles, speed, and danger—the breathtaking and deadly Isle of Man TT. The temporary race track used public roads for all its thirty-seven-point-seven-mile laps.

———

Molly came through the Sarah's Cottage corner, rear tire dinging the wet curb, the gutter full of slick rainwater and leaves. The bike wobbled. She corrected, not lifting off the throttle. Clicking off the gears, she got up to 230 km in the straightaway of sweepers before entering the Kirk Michael section for the next dizzying fast section of the race course.

She took the Handley bend running right up against the pasture wall of stacked stone, the field beyond dotted with herded sheep. The mist had worsened into a rain, her visor was blurred, the reduced view not slowing her up. The next section was all top-gear sweepers, leading into the tight turns of the Ramsey's section.

Coming out of the first hairpin, she let out a power slide for the pure joy, even though it slowed up her acceleration and her qualifying time.

"*Just like life*," she yelled inside her helmet, entering the next high-speed blast through a hard-paved roadway with unforgiving walls. The streaming set of sweepers was bringing her a familiar tunnel vision. She hit 290 km before a sideways braking into the next twisty section.

As the course continued to unfurl southward, the rain let up, replaced by a mist.

The rise on the pavement over an aqueduct launched her airborne again, both tires in the air for twenty long yards.

She braked too late for the Creg-ay-Baa turn and went through with the bike nearly lying down, her knee pad striking the street. Working throttle and brakes, she turned her wide-set handlebars in, catching the bike before it hit the low stone wall.

"*Yes!*" she screamed inside her padded helmet, a deep-from-the-spine laugh. The following tight and quick series of turns were rife with the *furniture* of stone walls, hay bales, and low buildings pressed to the edge of the public road. Closing in on the end of her second qualie lap, she worked each short straight and slick turn for all the speed she could find.

Finishing the lap, she entered the pits in view of the grandstands full of flags and fans.

She idle-rolled the bike through the crowd of team and course workers and press to her box where Allison waited. Swinging the bike in and shutting it off, she rocked it back onto its two-sided kickstand. Staring straight ahead, her hands were shaking, her knees trembling and bouncing.

Allison leaned over into her view and didn't say a word, leaving Molly to gather herself. Instead, he looked in the same direction to where competitors re-joined the course via the south ramp in Parc Ferme. It was a full minute before she raised her visor and looked to him. He spoke first.

"And?" he asked.

"Need brake balance moved forward. Five percent."

"And?"

"Scarier than birth."

"Gears?"

"No changes."

"Shocks?"

"Let's see how the brake bias works out first."

She climbed off the 1198cc Panigale R Ducati, the motor-cycled painted Italian red with a blue engine cowling void of sponsorship decals. The used bike was heavily modified, including her required wide-set *mustache* handlebars, often snickered at by other riders.

Pulling off her helmet, she looked to Allison with only her eyes showing from her black Nomex head sock. Standing in boots and leathers, she watched Allison roll over the toolbox to the front of the bike.

"The wrist?" he asked. The cast had come off three months after the Rick Ables, Jr. killing but still troubled her.

"It's good," her voice was muffled by the fireproof fabric.

"Your side?"

The head sock came off, and she shook out her hair, looking for a towel to rub her face with.

"Like it never happened. What was my time?"

"You're in. Buried in the pack but good."

Molly gave Allison a knife flick of a smile.

Stepping over to their toolboxes and parts crates, she

splashed bottled water on a rag and rubbed the creases on her face from the helmet. Returning to the bike, she kneeled beside Allison to watch him work his magic with the brakes.

He turned and grinned into her serious, focused, and lovely eyes.

"Your cell went off." He took her phone from his shirt pocket. "Interesting number."

There was a text message under a once-familiar number. She read it slowly, twice.

"Did you read it?" she asked Allison.

"Course not."

"Do."

He did, lowering his head after the last line.

After the pause, he went back to work, saying nothing,

Six minutes later, the front brake had been adjusted. Molly pulled the Nomex cap back on and took up her helmet resting on the Ducati's red fuel tank. She climbed aboard, and the two of them restarted the motorcycle.

Backing the bike off the jack, she prepared to burn in the rear tire.

As she was pulling on her helmet, Allison shouted, his hand gripping her shoulder for reassurance and balance.

"She's in a fine and better place."

Molly put her helmet on without a word. She dropped her visor with her eyes and thoughts focused forward.

CHAPTER 50

Three Fingers

Candy entered the cemetery as a midday tropical rain began, the winds spiraling wet leaves this way and that. She walked through the historical section, past ornate carved headstones and Gothic mausoleums from the 1700s. Poured footpaths led to the new section of modest markers that lay pressed flat in the lawn.

She sat down on a stone bench beside a massive old and strong oak tree. Before her was a view of the new section of internments.

"How are we doing?" she asked, not surprised when April didn't reply. April wasn't much for talking these days.

Candy was content to sit and watch.

April was wearing a white silk dress with tiny spring flowers on it. Her movements were stilted and lurching from the brain injury. She turned around slowly and looked around in all directions.

Candy watched her closely.

April hiked up her dress and squatted. She released a stream of urine on the marker between her ankles.

Rick Ables, Jr.
1988 – 2018

For the first time ever, Candy heard the delightfully rich sound of April's wicked laughter.

April crossed to her, hand out.

"My cell, please?" Her voice sounded as though her mouth was full of marbles.

Candy stood and pulled the phone from her pocket. April typed and sent her first text to Molly.

April: *Molly-girl, miss you. I'm happy we killed him. Still not right in the head. It's ok. Love, Three-fingers.*

Candy put the phone away and took April's arm. They walked slowly side by side, back up the paths to the front gates. April's stride wasn't hesitant but was restrained by her uncertain balance.

April's waiting Uber driver stood alongside his car, door open, umbrella raised. She waived away his and Candy's offers to help her climb inside.

"See you at home?" Candy asked.

April arched one brow, smiling.

"C'mon." Her voice was garbled and slow. "We've got money to steal."

The End

ACKNOWLEDGMENTS

Special Thanks to

Shakespeare Insult Kit by Jerry Maguire

Avi Selk – The Washington Post Hackers... 01/28/2018

ABOUT THE AUTHOR

Greg Jolley earned a Master of Arts in Writing from the University of San Francisco and lives in the very small town of Ormond Beach, Florida. When not writing, he researches historical crime, primarily those of the 1800s. Or goes surfing.

gfjolle@sbcglobal.net
www.TheDansers.com

ALSO BY GREG JOLLEY

Distractions

Danser

Dot to Dot

The Amazing Kazu

Murder in a Very Small Town

Where's Karen?

Malice in a Very Small Town

The Girl in the Hotel (as Gregory French)

View Finder

Black Veil

The Collectors

All of the Danser novels are available at: Amazon: http://amzn.to/204tIob

CPSIA information can be obtained
at www.ICGtesting.com
Printed in the USA
LVHW021030010221
677999LV00020B/337/J